Risk of Exposure

RISK OF EXPOSURE

Alpha Ops Book 6

EMMY CURTIS

New York   Boston

Copyright © 2016 by Emmy Curtis
Preview of *Compromised* copyright © 2016 by Emmy Curtis
Cover images © Shutterstock. Cover design by Elizabeth Turner.
Cover copyright © 2016 by Hachette Book Group, Inc.

Forever Yours
Hachette Book Group
1290 Avenue of the Americas
New York, NY 10104

forever-romance.com
twitter.com/foreverromance

First published as an ebook and as a print on demand: May 2016

Forever Yours is an imprint of Grand Central Publishing.

The Forever Yours name and logo are trademarks of Hachette Book Group, Inc.

The publisher is not responsible for websites (or their content) that are not owned by the publisher.

The Hachette Speakers Bureau provides a wide range of authors for speaking events. To find out more, go to www.hachettespeakersbureau.com or call (866) 376-6591.

ISBNs: 978-1-4555-3523-1 (ebook edition); 978-1-4555-6413-2 (print-on-demand edition)

E3

For the Chief, who keeps my heart warm.
And for Kora, who keeps my feet warm.

Acknowledgments

None of these Alpha Ops books would have been possible without my husband—who told me his combat stories and showed me that, regardless of what you might read in many romance books, you don't need to be a marine sniper or a member of the SEAL teams to be a true hero. So this series is for him, a USAF active duty chief master sergeant, who has deployed eight times in service of his country and has more medals than you can shake a really big stick at. I love you.

CHAPTER ONE

BARRACKS SECURITY SITREP

Officer: Malone Garrett

Principal: Abigail Baston

Ops Update: Baston is still unaware. Her days have a routine that anyone could follow. And I mean anyone. My grandmother for instance. Each day she goes for a three-mile run, drives to the orphanage, and returns home.

I have been able to raise my skill level in Candy Crush, though, so I try to look on the bright side. I'm on level 1038 now. I'm a fucking genius at this. Have you tried it? I have to say, though, if I have to stay here much longer, the skills you really hired me for will be dormant. So...sorry about that. And that's the British "sorry." The one that means that I'm not sorry because it's all your fault.

Date of completion: Level 1039 here I come.

> ˙Wasn't sure if you'd understand that finer detail in print, so I thought I'd better explain. Probably made it less funny, didn't it?

He hit ENTER and then had a pang of…something. He'd sworn to himself that he wouldn't make fun of his boss's concern about his daughter, but fifteen reports later and it was frankly too hard to keep a lid on his frustration. The sooner his boss realized that she was safe, the sooner Mal could go on to his next job—which would hopefully be more interesting than following the most bloody boring woman in the world around the most bloody boring town in Ukraine.

Abby Baston was one of life's do-gooders. She'd dropped out of college in her first semester to join Aide Internationale and was currently working at a Ukrainian orphanage. She'd been there about six months, and her father was getting increasingly concerned for her safety, after the recent saber rattling of the Russians.

Mal's instructions were to get her out if the Russians did anything aggressive, like storming the Ukrainian border. Of course the silly woman had chosen an orphanage less than five klicks from the Russian border.

And, of course, Mal was spinning his wheels, following her sorry arse around: apartment, run, apartment, orphanage, and apartment again. He wanted to shout at her to get a fucking life. Go somewhere interesting, do something dubious—anything to make this job less boring. She barely smiled or broke stride to even look in a shop window.

And it was fucking hard work, sitting there doing nothing. Under normal circumstances, he'd just engineer a meeting, seduce her, and pretend to be her boyfriend until the job was over. It was a method he'd perfected over time, and by far the easiest way to keep an unsuspecting principal close and safe.

Not to mention the most fun. But she wasn't interesting enough to warrant even entertaining that idea.

Besides, he valued his job. Baston was one of the few people who didn't bat an eye at Mal's heavily redacted employment record. So this was a job worth keeping, and seducing the boss's daughter was out of the question. Which meant that he actually had to do his job and follow her everywhere she went. And now his life was effectively as boring as hers.

He checked that the sitrep had been received, checked his watch and yawned, leaned back in his plastic lawn chair, and propped his feet on the windowsill of his apartment. A camera was set up on a tripod, for all the good it did. The girl closed the curtains when she came home from the orphanage at night. He sighed and closed his eyes. He'd never been as tired on a job as he was here.

There was just nothing to keep his brain occupied. In the two weeks he'd been in the flat, he'd tried crosswords, sudoku, and mahjong. He hadn't actually tried Candy Crush. He was saving that as a last resort. Even his damn PC was complaining at the shit he was making it do. A quiet buzzer went off beside him and he reluctantly took his feet off the sill and leaned forward, his hand on the remote for the camera.

He'd put the alarm under the carpet in her doorway so that

he'd be alerted to anyone entering her flat. Even if it was just her. He checked his watch again. Yup. She was bang on time.

His boss was a wizened old dog who had any number of awful and awesome stories to tell after a drink and a cigar. What the hell had happened to his offspring? His son was some kind of corporate lawyer and his daughter was…well, an aid worker. Where was this generation's love of danger, excitement, and risk?

Okay, it wasn't exactly a different generation; she was only six years younger than him. But still. He leaned back in his rickety chair and contemplated the women he'd had who'd been about six years younger. And then he wondered what Danielle was up to now—she'd been every bit of six years older than him…and those six years were all she'd admitted to. But she'd been a classy—and very dirty—lady. He grinned at the memory. They'd been in the Sinai; he'd been collecting intel, and she did work for the embassy. She'd opened doors for him in Egyptian society that would have remained closed to someone like him. She was—

What the…

He got up so fast that the lawn chair snapped closed and fell to the floor. Abby was opening the window, despite the chilly evening air. She was jumping up and down. What the…?

The floor-to-ceiling windows showed virtually all her apartment except the bedroom, which he'd already looked at the first time he'd broken in. He grinned as she waved her hands around. She'd burned something. Ouch, looked like it had spilled down her. For a second something panged in him, seeing her with red all down her shirt. A wafer-thin sliver of his brain thought she might've been shot, but the rest of his brain's experience reminded him that gunshot victims rarely flapped around like that.

For a second something else flickered across his mind. That tiny sliver of his brain hadn't been surprised at the prospect of her being shot. Mal's eyes flickered to the right for a second as he tried to solidify that thought. There was something about her. Was anyone really that dull in real life? Especially a relative of his boss? Was she hiding something?

He'd survived years of combat and enemy activity just listening to his gut. And his gut was now singing a song that had been alien to him before Abby had spilled tomato sauce down her front. Accepting that maybe she wasn't exactly as she seemed relaxed him. It was as if his instinct had been waiting for his brain to catch up. He was going to have to meet her.

Somehow.

Eyes on Abby, he opened a bag of strangely flavored Ukrainian crisps…no chance of burning anything in here. He hadn't even touched the kitchen—such as it was—since he'd arrived. He watched the windows of her apartment, newly alert to any possibility.

She disappeared for a few minutes, and he picked up his binoculars.

He looked back up as a movement caught his eye. She'd taken her shirt off and was waving it around her head, trying to get the smoke out of the apartment. In her underwear. He fumbled the binoculars and they fell on his foot. He winced and picked them up, carefully stretching his foot to make sure there was no lasting damage.

Looking across the road, he could still see her waving the smoke away. His fingers twitched toward the binoculars again. Every cell in his body wanted to see her in her underwear, but he knew he shouldn't.

Except…he had a hook in his brain now. Something wasn't right. He just couldn't figure out what.

He peered through the window. Yes, he could have gone all zoom lens on her, but knowing she was in her underwear kind of made him feel sketchy about looking. All he needed to do was make sure she was okay and try to figure out what was starting to bother him about her.

She was laughing at herself. Waving her arms around the room like a crazy person. He smiled. He'd seen her smile only a couple of times, and once had been in an ID photo that was in her file.

Bloody Nora.

She started dancing like a crazy person, still wafting smoke out the window. She wriggled out of her skirt and started wafting that around her head, making her look like she was twirling duo lassos from a distance. It was like watching a totally different person. In virtually no clothes. He looked away again, but his eyes were inevitably drawn back to the tableau.

She coughed, covering her mouth with her skirt, and he tensed. Was there gas? Was the smoke too much for her? But she just turned back to the kitchen. Then she popped open a few other windows and continued waving her arms to get rid of the residual burning smell probably, laughing and singing, seemingly at the top of her voice. This was totally not the Abby he'd been following for weeks. Not even close. She looked fun.

She also looked okay. Determined not to invade her privacy anymore, he grabbed his phone and paged through the news. A flash from Abby's window caught his eye and he looked up again. She was closing the windows and swishing the curtains shut. All but one that didn't go all the way. He watched for a second and then went back to the news—such as it was. Celebrities, politics, and wars. He sighed and clicked through to a story about the G20 meetings that were being held in Athens. He knew a few operatives working there, so he scanned the article for anything familiar.

He took one more cursory look at Abby's apartment.

Oh my God, what is she doing now? This was obviously a part of her evening routine that he hadn't seen before.

Abby stretched like a cat, yawned, and held some kind of yoga pose. He saw only half her body between the curtains that hadn't completely shut, but still, he couldn't help but notice her breasts move together as she did.

He swallowed. Look away, look away.

He looked back.

She turned around and touched her toes. Jesus fucking Christ. Impossibly small panties covered barely anything. His eyes flicked to the binoculars. *No way, Garrett.* He wasn't going to start being a Peeping Tom at this advanced age. God, he wanted to see her, though. What did that make him?

And did he really care?

It was like seeing her with a whole new perspective. Okay, she was almost naked, but still—he had to find out more about her, if only to quell his gut. He started to second-guess himself. Was he reaching for an excuse to actually meet her? Was he fooling himself into believing he had a gut feeling that something wasn't as it seemed?

He looked again, resolutely leaving the binoculars on the floor.

He was a fucking saint.

Her wavy dark hair was pinned up in some kind of bun, and the reading glasses she wore seriously made Mal think he was watching *True Confessions of a Librarian Behind Closed Doors*. There must be a reality show like that somewhere in the world.

Between the swaying curtains that half hid her, she slid gently and slowly into the splits. She bent and touched her arms to her left foot, and then to her right, and then to her left again.

She brought her legs together in front of her and stood. Turning so her back was toward the window, she swung her arms around, holding each shoulder with her other hand, as if they were sore. Rolling her neck from side to side, she took out whatever was holding her hair up and let the curls fall down her back.

His mouth went dry. She was beautiful. Not her hair, or face, or body—although now that he was getting a good look, he couldn't deny their allure—but it was her grace that really took a hold of him. It was as if there were two Abbys. The one who never cracked a smile, who followed a precise routine and never seemed as if she was capable of fun. The other could laugh at herself, even when the kitchen was on fire. She danced and sang and laughed. And then the way she held her arms, the legs that were obviously as strong as they were long. How her back looked when she stretched, long muscles moving under her skin.

He wondered what her skin felt like.

And wondered why he'd briefly thought it normal that she might have been shot.

She turned back to the window and reached behind her back as if she were about to take off her bra. He stood, stock-still, almost holding his breath. But her head jerked to the side, and she stopped what she was doing and picked up the phone from a sofa cushion.

Damn that caller to hell. Damn him.

He took a breath, realizing he was as hard as he'd ever been, not actually physically touching someone.

He wanted to meet her. To explore his gut feeling about her. Sure. That was why.

Abby closed the curtains all the way, suddenly realizing that if anyone in the opposite building was home, which judging by the lack of lights didn't look possible, they'd be able to see straight into her apartment, and probably judge her for her lack of cooking skills. To be honest, it could only loosely be called cooking.

How do you burn tomato soup? Then, how was it possible to move it so fast from the stove that it slopped over onto your only white blouse? She had no idea what was up with her today, but cooking was not in the cards. The smoke had already blackened the ceiling over the stove and she wondered for a second what would happen if the CIA couldn't get their deposit back. She snorted softly to herself. Drone strike? A visit from "the guys"?

The smoke had left the apartment, leaving a sweet charred

smell that she hoped would also dissipate soon. Good thing she wasn't fieldstripping guns or having to pass aptitude tests. She'd been so clumsy recently. She was out of practice. With everything.

She'd had this insane idea that someone had been watching her, but she'd never seen anyone, and no one had intercepted her when she left to dead-drop information under the guise of going for a run. She'd looked for a good week before deciding that she was imagining it. The problem with being a covert officer—a solitary profession at the best of times—was that it made you slightly paranoid. Sometimes correctly, but most often not.

She stretched again and grinned to herself as she turned on the water in the shower. She never imagined she'd be given a job so dull that an imaginary tail would be a welcome distraction. Regardless, the Russian border and whoever crossed it was her only focus.

The orphanage—her cover—held a surveillance point, what she called her little watchtower, so she could keep her eye on the border.

She was just north of the "Russian-backed fighters" and the Ukrainians, who were having sporadic firefights in the towns and countryside. Thing was—no one knew if the fighters were really "Russian-backed" or if they were part of Russia's legitimate army. If it was the latter and Abby could get proof, then the might of NATO's combined armies would converge to get Ukraine's back. It was probably the most important job she'd ever been given and she was going to effing ace it. Even if her hosts were less than impressed that she was there.

She switched off the water and stood staring at the shower wall for a second. For these six months, she'd only had contact with her landlord, Tanoff, and his disapproving wife, Brigda. Well, and the kids in the orphanage, but that didn't really count since she was somewhat rusty on the hybrid Ukrainian/Russian that they spoke in the area.

Six long months on her own. She wanted to talk to someone. Just to see if she could smile still. If those muscles even worked. She wanted to touch someone. Even if it was an accidental brush of fingers.

As she dried her hair, she practiced smiling in the mirror. It was pitiful. Fake, and not to put too fine a point on it, it looked as if it pained her to smile.

Once, she'd worked from the US embassy in Moscow. She'd arrived in winter and the first thing she'd noticed was that no one smiled. Not in the street, not in the stores, not even in the embassy. It was as if an air of suppression rested on everyone in the country. An arctic freeze, she supposed. Only vodka brought smiles. And that was only if it was the good stuff. And those smiles only lasted until the bottle became empty. It was the same here. She blamed the proximity to the Russian border.

Maybe she'd go out tomorrow night. To that bar a few streets away that she passed on her way to the orphanage. She'd double-check the street name on her way to work tomorrow. Even if she only spoke to the bartender, it would be one more person on her scant list of contacts that she was supposed to fill out daily. She hated to think just how boring the analysts at Langley must think her. Or maybe she'd go to the restaurant she'd been to a couple of times when she'd had no food in the house. Whatever she did, she needed to socialize with someone. Anyone.

She suspected that her clumsiness, her off-center feeling, wasn't coming from Russia but from her complete isolation.

Maybe she could pick a fight at the bar. If she had to punch someone to get skin-on-skin contact, she'd take that too. Fighting might be the closest contact she'd have had with another human being since— Crap, how long had it been? Maybe three years?

And that was nothing to sniff at.

CHAPTER TWO

Mal awoke to the familiar sound of a jackhammer outside his window. There were no noise ordinances in this town, and he'd basically started to use the noise as a morning alarm. Sometimes they started at six; sometimes it was closer to nine. He suspected it was down to the amount of vodka consumed the night before, and once or twice he'd considered dropping off a crate of booze for them when he needed a lie-in.

Abigail Baston didn't usually leave until eight, so he still had—he looked at his cell phone—half an hour before he had to be in his car. A combat shower and a cup of instant coffee with hot tap water only set him back five minutes, so he stretched and thought about the previous night. He visualized her with the red stains on her shirt and tried to organize his initial gut reaction into something solid. What had changed?

He didn't think it was the guy she worked with at the orphanage—he was married to a terrifyingly stern-looking woman. No one in his right mind would mess with her. And Abby hadn't crossed paths with anyone else in the three weeks he'd been there.

Stretching on the thin mattress he'd bought and thrown on the floor when he rented the apartment, Mal went over her last day again. Nope. There had been nothing.

He closed his eyes and went through her routine again. So ordinary. So boring. Was it planned that way? Was she deliberately being routine-driven so as to lull anyone watching into a stupor? He sighed. If so, it had definitely worked. His mind shifted to her dancing around her apartment wafting smoke away with her blouse and skirt. He smiled. It was a different side to her, an appealing side.

He heaved himself up, and as estimated, in ten minutes he was showered, dressed, and working on being caffeinated.

His job was surveillance, but that didn't mean he was following her every minute of the day. He basically checked in with her, making sure she was approximately where she was supposed to be when she was supposed to be there. Although from time to time he did follow her on her three-mile run, to the store, and to the orphanage, mostly he just sat back making sure no one else was watching her.

Why did his boss think someone might be watching her? At first he thought it was a normal daddy paranoia—not having kids, or anyone that he felt close to, Mal had no frame of reference for that—but maybe it wasn't? He shook his head at himself. He was going to meet with her and assess her that way. If nothing twanged his Spidey sense, then he was going to go hard with his campaign to get off this case. Or lack-of-case. But right now—it was back to following her.

In truth, most people could tell when they were being watched. Whether they consciously understood it or not, some little voice whispered unease to them. And that was definitely not his intention with Baston's daughter. Uneasy people did stupid things, and he had no desire to push her into any trouble that he'd have to extricate her from.

He got in his 1986 maroon Škoda and made his way out of town, about one klick away from the orphanage, where he parallel parked outside a used car lot and sat there, watching for her own Škoda to pass.

It did, and Mal sighed. Half relief, half sadness that this woman was so predictable. He felt very sorry for her. But that wasn't his problem. In fact, the more boring her life, the faster he could return to doing a proper job.

God, he hoped Baston didn't keep him here indefinitely to look out for his daughter. If only she'd given him an opportunity to hit on her, this long wait to be reassigned would have been easy. And probably fun. Yup, even though she was Baston's daughter, if he'd become her friend, maybe even kissed her, it would have lightened the job somewhat. As it was, it was probably going to be the death of him.

Fuck this. He'd been watching her for three weeks and had seen her smile exactly twice. Once through a zoom lens when one of the orphans broke out of the house to welcome her and once last night. He'd watched, squinting, as the little kid had run into her arms. She'd smiled, once, and that one smile had chipped a sliver of ice from his cold, black heart. Then last night. He'd seen her bra, goddammit. Fuck this all to hell. He was going to meet her, come hell or high water. Screw Baston. He wanted out of this crazy assignment.

It was going to happen today. He had eight hours to figure out how.

Abby played with Lana, the little three-year-old, brown-eyed girl, while World War III raged in the kitchen. Tanoff and Brigda were arguing *again* about harboring an American. Well, to be more precise, an American government employee. That's as much as the CIA liaison had told them when he'd handed over enough cash to keep the orphanage, and the children, going for a few years.

Brigda wasn't happy about the arrangement, wanted more money for the perceived danger or wanted Abby gone. Tanoff was pleading with her not to do anything stupid. Abby's ears pricked up. She'd never told them that she understood their language. Enough people in this part of Ukraine spoke English. Right now she was happy she hadn't let on. But if he was talking her out of doing something stupid, then they must have already discussed maybe turning her in to the authorities.

The couple's older son was a member of the local police. More like a town sheriff. He was a good-looking young man whose eyes had lit up when he'd met the American aid worker who was volunteering at his parents' orphanage. But she had no doubt he would arrest her if Brigda voiced any suspicions about her to him. The problem with that part of Ukraine was that you could never be sure about anyone's allegiance. He could be a Russian sympathizer, wanting to reintegrate with the mother country, or he could be a fierce separatist. Either way, if Brigda broke the confidentiality clause in the contract, all their money would disappear, and the orphanage would effectively be shut down. Abby didn't want that either.

She listened until the argument wore itself out. She had a hunch that Tanoff knew that Aide Internationale was a front for the CIA. Why else would he get paid for taking in a volunteer? But she also sensed that he didn't mind.

She carefully put Lana into her high chair as the eleven other children came running in from different parts of the farmhouse.

"No, no, no. Wash your hands first," she chided. She motioned hand washing and pointed to the sink in the corner of the room, and they all lined up, taking turns stepping on the upturned crate she'd placed there so they could reach the soap and faucet. One by one, they stepped down and held their hands out to Abby so she could dry their little fingers with a towel. Secretly she reveled in the feel of their tiny trusting hands in hers. Half of her wished she were only here to help at the orphanage, that she had no ulterior motive that kept her up at night. No reason for Brigda to be suspicious of her and no reason to fear being sent to prison for spying.

The children took their seats around the table, and she kissed the heads closest to her before she slipped into her North Face jacket. Tanoff barreled into the room with plates, shouting, "Who's hungry?" with a broad smile across his face.

Hands went up and shouts of "Me!" filled the room along with loud giggles.

Tanoff caught her eye. "You should go. Have some fun in town." His eyes twinkled as she rolled her eyes.

"Sure thing!" She buttoned her jacket and grabbed her backpack.

"Drive with safety," he said, placing plates in front of the rowdy children.

"I always do," she replied as she did every day. "See you tomorrow."

He smiled and nodded, directing his attention to little Leonid, who was tugging at his sleeve.

She felt an unusual tingle in her spine as she started the engine in her wreck of a car. She looked into the dusk and saw nothing. No movement in the farm, other than the animals. Nothing in the fields. Maybe she was just slightly unnerved by the fight she'd overheard.

Five minutes into her short drive home, she passed another old beater Škoda with its hood up. She slowed down. It was pointing the opposite way, so it wasn't like she could really offer him a ride. She was about to pass it, when she caught sight of the man, or more specifically, his jacket. It was bright red and emblazoned with MEDCIN SANS FRONTIERS. She pulled over. She wasn't going to strand a fellow aid worker in the countryside at night.

"Ca va?" she asked.

"Eh. I've been better," he replied in a deep voice with a distinct English accent.

"And you're not French," she said, slamming her door and striding over to him.

"Not even a little bit." He straightened and blew out a sigh as he held his hand out to her. "Malone Garrett. Thanks for stopping."

She shook his hand and looked into the engine. "Anything I can help with?"

He cocked his head and looked down at her.

A jolt of awareness flashed through her as he met her eyes. He was all man. Firm jaw, really blue eyes, way over six feet, and built to match. His jean-clad legs were long and clearly muscled. She suddenly wanted to see what was under his jacket and shirt…Her long-dormant libido kick-started in her stomach, sending unwelcome messages through her body. *Jesus, girl. Get a grip.*

"Are you good with cars?" he asked, a hint of a smile behind his words.

I can hot-wire them, siphon fuel from them, disable them, make them explode, and change a fan belt, but aside from that, not really.

"I'm good at giving stranded motorists rides back into town," she said, as if she was admitting she knew nothing about cars.

"In which case, I'd be grateful to take advantage of that skill, if you don't mind," he said, closing the hood. He got back into his car, turned off the headlights, and grabbed a messenger bag from the backseat.

She got back in her car and watched him in her rearview mirror. His accent did strange things to her. Maybe it was just speaking to someone who actually spoke English as a first language. Maybe it was something different. Holy hell. Did God send him because she'd been determined to meet someone? Or at least touch someone?

He opened the door and peered in. "Are you sure? I promise

I'm not an ax murderer." He smiled disarmingly, and for a second she considered that that was precisely what an ax murderer would say. She shrugged to herself. Anything to relieve the boredom of her life.

"Sure. Maybe you should be asking if I'm the ax murderer?"

A frown flickered across his face for a second and she laughed. "I'm not, I promise."

He got in and put his seat belt on. "Isn't that exactly what an ax murderer would say, though?"

She laughed again. "You're the one who brought up ax murderers. Maybe I kill with a spork. Maybe you're making me feel inferior with all your talk about axes." She pulled onto the road and headed toward the flickering lights of the town about thirteen miles away.

"Then let's drop the subject. Although, clearly, axes are superior in that line of business."

She sniffed. "You haven't seen what I can do with a spork."

He laughed, a low belly laugh. "So perhaps I can take you out to dinner, to thank you for your assistance this evening. That way, I can see firsthand how proficient you are with cutlery."

"Perhaps you can." She bit her lip from jumping on the offer but couldn't stop a smile spreading across her face.

"So what is an American girl like you doing in the Ukrainian countryside?" he asked, pushing his messenger bag from his lap and onto the floor.

"There's an orphanage about four miles away from where you broke down. I work there. What about you?"

"I do tech support for NGOs in this region. I must have got turned around."

"You must have. There's nothing at the end of that road except a couple of villages and Russia. I'm not sure you should venture so close to the border."

"I'm not so worried about that. I can take care of myself."

"Even against a strange aid worker wielding a spork?" she asked with a grin.

"I guess we'll just have to wait and see, won't we?"

CHAPTER THREE

Where would you like me to drop you?" she asked, slowing down at the outskirts of the town.

"Wherever you recommend we go for dinner. I haven't eaten all day and I'm starving." He knew full well that she was in two minds about going to eat with him, so he framed his answer in a way that it was a foregone conclusion.

"Don't worry." She flashed a smile at him. "I wasn't planning on ditching you. We'll go eat. I'm looking forward to seeing how impressive you are with a spoon. Honestly, it's all I can think about. I just didn't know if you wanted to go to your hotel first." She frowned. "Or…wait, do you have a hotel here, or are you staying in another town?"

"I'm staying here. Close to the town center. I still don't exactly know where everything is yet, though. I've only been here a few days." Kind of the truth at least.

"Oh, well certainly you need to see the splendor of the

tobacco shop on Sebastopol—it dates back to the 1980s, I believe. Also the supermarket that only sells vodka and sardines should certainly be on your sightseeing itinerary. There's so much to do around here."

He laughed. She was as funny in person as she had been in her apartment the previous day. Such a departure from the previous two weeks he'd been watching her. "Not a great town?" he asked.

"It's actually not bad. Everyone is quite friendly, and you can get what you need, if not always what you want."

"How very Rolling Stones of you," he said, looking out into the darkness. There was nothing out here—no lights, no nothing. He could just as well be gazing out to a dark sea. Good to know.

"How long are you in the country for?" she asked, using her indicator absurdly late, and turning into a broad tree-lined road with streetlights.

As long as you are, probably. "Undecided. It all depends on my boss," he said. "What about you?"

They pulled up in front of what looked like an old sewing machine store and she turned off the engine. "Ditto."

"Are we here?" He looked around and saw nothing that could be construed as a restaurant.

"Trust me. You've got to really want something here to find it." She shoved her hands into her jeans pockets, her long brown hair slightly unkempt, and all the more sexy for it, looking like temptation.

Like wicked, wicked temptation. He should have known that meeting her was a bad idea. He should have known that he'd like her. He should have known to keep away. "Lead on," he said.

"You're very trusting," she said, nodding up an alley and then leading the way. "I could be leading you into a den of organized crime and terrorists."

"Frankly, at this stage, as long as they fed me, I wouldn't even care."

A gratifying chuckle floated back in the cold air.

At the end of the alley, there was a metal door; the only sign was a tiny plaque with Cyrillic lettering on it. She yanked open the door and took the metal stairs two at a time. Maybe she *was* taking him somewhere sketchy.

By the time they'd reached the second landing, he could hear voices and clinking of plates and glasses. She opened another metal door and stood back for him to enter. He laughed. "How did you ever find this place?"

For all the metal doors and stairs, the huge room was decked out like an Alpine lodge, wooden floors, walls, and ceilings, with thick wooden bench tables. The smell of food and beer almost brought him to his knees. In the short time he'd been in country, he'd found only snack foods at the train station.

"The owner of the orphanage recommended it. He used to come here all the time with his family. Hans, the guy who owns the restaurant, is the third generation to run it. Everyone in town knows this place—and out-of-towners don't. Which suits everyone quite well."

The guy behind the bar looked exactly how a Hans should look: tall, beefy, with hands the size of frying pans.

She held up her hand to get Hans's attention and then pointed at a free table. He nodded at her, but his eyes were on Mal.

"Are you going to be in trouble for bringing an outsider here?" he asked, taking a seat opposite her.

"Probably, but I'm a risk taker." She grinned, took her leather jacket off, and shivered. "Surprising how cold it can get here so early in the year, isn't it?"

"Why don't you keep your jacket on, then?" he asked, still wondering about the trouble she thought may be coming.

"The food I'm ordering is hot. Super hot. Trust me," she said.

"I have no idea why I keep trusting you, but okay. I'm in your hands. All evening." Dammit, why had he said that?

"Good to know, Malone. Good to know." She leaned back and tilted her head. "So why are you here again? How long have you been here, and where did you come in from?"

"Wow. You kiss the Spanish Inquisition with that mouth?" He smiled.

She laughed, tipping her head back, showing the creamy, smooth skin of her neck. He wondered what she smelled like. What she tasted like. *Shit, Mal. She's Baston's daughter. Take it down a notch.*

Hans rumbled to the table and brought two beers with what looked like vodka chasers. "Raclette?" he asked.

"Please," she said. "Hans, this is my brother, Malone."

What? What the fuck? He fished around in his repertoire for an American accent that sounded approximately like Baston's. "Pleasure to meet you," he said, standing and holding out his hand.

Hans's face broke into a wide smile as he shook hands with Mal. "Indeed, indeed. Welcome to you, sir."

"Thank you." He retook his seat as Hans bustled off. "What was that all about?"

She shrugged. "Hans is a lovely man, and he likes me. I didn't want to admit that I'd picked up a man on the side of the road—a man I know nothing about—and brought him to his restaurant. He would worry. Now he won't worry."

He sat back in admiration. "Wow, you can lie really well. I mean, it just came out of you, no hesitation, no planning. *Are you a sociopath?*"

She downed her shot of vodka in one and it could have been water for the reaction she showed. "I don't know. I've never been tested. Maybe." She raised her eyebrows at him as she took a sip of the frothy beer. "Then again, you're the one who came up with the accent in a split second. Nicely done, by the way. Are you sure you're not American, just pretending to be all mysterious and British?"

He laughed and took a longer swig of beer. He set the glass down and laced his hands on the table. "So, tell me again why I'm mysterious and sexy?"

"I didn't say sexy."

"But I know that's what you meant." He shouldn't be doing this; there was no way of getting around it. She was sexy, intelligent, and funny. Why couldn't he have a little fun? *Because of Baston.*

Before she could reply, their dinner arrived. Even though he wasn't quite as hungry as he'd claimed to be, his mouth watered at the sight of the food being piled on the table. Chunks of white bread, cold meats, and steaming potatoes and a contraption he'd never seen before. "Torture device?" he asked.

"Ve have vays of making you talk," she said in a passable circa World War II German accent. "It's a cheese melter. Watch."

Hans came back with a half round of cheese that he impaled on a spike. He moved around a hot grill so it was about an inch from the face of the cheese. "*Smačnoho*," he said as he left to attend to another table.

"*Diakuju*," she replied, thanking him.

Mal watched as Abby put a potato, a slice of meat, and a cornichon on her plate. Then she scraped melted cheese onto her plate and started eating. She paused as her first forkful approached her mouth. "I thought you were hungry?" She slid the food into her mouth and closed her eyes briefly as she savored the dish.

"Oh, I am," he said, eyes on her mouth. *Shut up. Shut your bloody mouth.*

She gestured to Hans for more vodka and nodded toward the food as she took another mouthful.

He started piling food onto his plate, and when he took his first bite, he understood Abby's initial, eyes-closed appreciation. "How have I not had this before?" he asked between mouthfuls.

"Hmmm," she said, dabbing her napkin on her mouth. "You were a poor, deprived child, slightly nervous. Never wanted to rock the boat until you found yourself in an institution. Boy Scouts? Boarding school? Juvenile detention? Military? Who knows? But as soon as you got there, you didn't like any of the rules, and you became addicted to breaking them. You've never done anything conventional, like being in a relationship, taking vacations, going skiing, eating raclette, because that would make you feel constrained, bound by rules. You're a lone wolf, destined to roam alone." She paused. "Or, you know, you've never been to the Alps."

He nearly choked on his mouthful. She was right about nearly all of that. Nearly. "Oh my God, that was amazing. You nailed absolutely *nothing* there. I mean, I thought you'd have picked up one thing, maybe just by pure luck, but nice try." He tipped his refilled shot glass at her and clinked her glass.

"So weird. I keep thinking if I say that to all the men I meet, I'll be right at least one time. I guess you're not the right guy." He could have sworn that her smile was seductive. Like she was thinking something impossibly naughty. Or was that just wishful thinking?

Okay, he wasn't going to make a move, but if she made a move on him, he'd totally go with it. He made the deal with himself, not knowing which way he hoped it would go. Definitely knowing which way he wanted it to go. They ate in silence for a bit, but when the immediate need of sustenance was satisfied, he put his fork down and leaned forward, elbows on the table.

"So tell me about yourself. What gives you the guts to pick up a strange man on the side of the road, close to nighttime, in a foreign country? Or was it not guts but a death wish?" he asked, leaning back and almost groaning with the amount of cheese he'd eaten.

She took a sip of her drink this time and pushed her plate away. "I prefer to consider it good karma to help people in need. That's all. Don't you like to help people?"

"Not really, no. Not unless I know them. Not unless there's a good reason," he said honestly.

"Wow. That makes you kind of hard-hearted, doesn't it?" She smiled into her glass.

"Why would anyone want to be thought of as softhearted? Although I am extremely thankful for your incredibly soft…heart." He grinned as she nearly choked on her beer.

"Will you be able to get someone out there to fix your car in the morning?" she asked after clearing her throat.

"I'm sure I passed a workshop on the way out of town this morning. I'll just walk up there tomorrow. No rush."

"Well, I'm not going to offer you a ride since you derided my softheartedness. So you'll have to manage on your own." She finished her drink. "Do you want another one?"

He slugged back the remainder of his vodka and was about to say yes when she continued.

"My place or yours?"

It was his turn to choke.

She laughed, a glorious, rich laugh that seemed to come from her soul. *Her soul?* He looked at his glass. That was some fine alcohol right there.

"Are you up for it?" she asked frankly.

"Up for what?" He was still trying to clear his throat from the burn of the vodka and catch up with the direction the evening was taking.

She tipped her head. She put some local currency on the table and shrugged into her coat. "Well if you don't know, then I guess I have my answer."

She was already at the door by the time he'd collected his jacket and his wits. If she was offering what he thought she was offering, then according to his earlier deal with himself, he could fuck the hell out of her without worrying about the repercussions. It was the universe telling him he could. He was sure.

"Wait a minute," he said as soon as the door closed behind them. "What if I do know?"

She turned back, face mere inches from his. "Let's go to your place."

He leaned in and kissed her, pressing her up against the metal door and tasting the burning vodka still in her mouth. Her tongue stroked his, and his world tilted on its axis. He pulled away, his mouth millimeters away from hers.

"I don't like people in my space. Let's go to yours." It was the truth, although more pressing was the surveillance equipment directed at her apartment window.

"I don't like people in *my* space."

They were silent for a moment. She opened her mouth to speak when a family came out of the restaurant door. He jumped away from her—realizing instantly that it probably wouldn't do to be found French-kissing his sister with a hard-on the size of Big Ben.

"Come," she said, and started running up the metal stairs toward the roof.

The roof he could work with.

CHAPTER FOUR

This was like all her dreams come true. She'd been so desperate for company, for some human interaction. But this man, so handsome, and big, and *oh my God* the smell of him, all man and musk. She'd wanted him since they chatted in the car. Since he sparred verbally with her over dinner. She watched him tear at the bread with his huge hands and listened to him speak with his James Bond accent.

She just wanted him. For today, for now. He was a perfect distraction. Just passing through and kissed like a god, and she would lay money on the fact that he was just as skilled in other areas too. She couldn't tell if he had turned her knees to butter or if it had been the liquor, but either way, she wanted the fuck out of him. And she'd never have to see him again.

She opened the door to the roof, where Hans set out tables when it was warmer. There was nowhere to sit except the wall surrounding the rooftop.

As soon as she stopped to look at the town beneath them, he grabbed her arm and spun her around. His mouth crashed down on hers without warning. She opened her mouth under him, wanting to feel the urgency of the kiss. His tongue moved in her mouth like he already knew how to slay her. Her breath heaved in and out as she held him as tight as she could.

She needed this. She needed a release, some semblance of human closeness. He pulled her head back with her hair, and she moaned as his mouth sucked and bit at her neck. She slid her jacket off, despite the cold air. Heat was flowing through her like she was the Torch.

"You're fucking glorious, you know that?" he said in a gravelly voice. "I can't wait to be inside you, watching your eyes as I make you come."

A dirty talker too. Her hormones went into overdrive. She gasped for air as he yanked her head back to be kissed again. His hand slipped under her T-shirt and without stopping she pulled away from him and held her arms up. He slid the shirt off and lifted her so she could wrap her legs around him. His mouth went to her nipple, sucking and biting it through her bra.

She shivered and he put her down. "Are you too cold?" he rasped.

Not fucking likely. She reached behind her and took off her bra, allowing him to see her, wanting him to see her. His darkening eyes made her stomach clench with need.

"Jesus, you're beautiful." He swallowed visibly and dragged her to him again. This time he bit and pulled at her nipples until they were so hard they were virtually throbbing in the cold night air.

Not stopping to ask, or to say anything else, he ripped open the button on her jeans and dragged them halfway down her thighs. His hand plunged between her legs, under her panties, his large fingers diving into her folds.

"You're so wet. So fucking wet. How long have you been wet?"

"Since we sat down for dinner," she said, and then felt compelled to keep speaking. "I knew I wanted you right then, and the seam of my jeans was so perfectly placed for pressure..."

He groaned as his fingers played in her wetness. He pressed against her clitoris and she squirmed against him, needing more friction. Her hands reached for his jeans. She undid them and found he went commando. His dick was already hard and strong. "Do you have a condom?" she asked as she stroked him. "If you don't, I—"

"I've got one," he groaned as her fist tightened around the head of his dick.

She couldn't wait. "I need you inside me." She slid her jeans down a little farther, and as she bent to do so, she slid him into her mouth. He went completely still.

"If you keep doing that, I'm going to come. If you want me to fuck you, you better get back up here," he said.

She stood and turned away from him, looking over her shoulder at him as she put her hands on the wall. His hand slowly slid from her neck to her ass, and as he reached there, he pushed into her. Hard and fast, using her wetness. She half rose with the feeling of being so totally impaled. She moaned, heat pulsing out from her body as he thrust into her. He pulled her closer to him, one arm around her breasts, fingers pinching her nipple, and the other around her hips, sliding his fingers against her clit.

She felt her orgasm start from the pit of her stomach, arching toward her and ebbing away, only to reemerge again, stronger. As he pushed into her, her nipple and clit seemed to join with the rhythm of his fingers.

"Oh God," she breathed, and then spasmed as the hot wave crashed around her, jerking against him. He shook off his restraint and came, almost roaring with the intensity.

As soon as the warmth in her body started to dissipate, she waited for the shame to kick in. She pulled her jeans up and tugged her T-shirt and jacket back on, barely acknowledging his presence. When she was ready to go, she stood up straight and looked him in the eye. She smiled involuntarily at his confusion, then realized she felt zero shame.

"Thanks, I needed that," she said, almost urging the surge of shame and embarrassment to come.

"Glad I could assist?" he said, frowning with what seemed like uncertainty.

"Can you find your way back to your hotel?" she asked, reaching for the door. Why wasn't she feeling anything except satiation and calm and…peace? Should she stay? Indulge in a little more small talk? She could. But if she were to go now, she would have a perfect memory of him. She didn't want to spoil the moment finding out that he was a jerk or, worse, a Yankees fan or something. She paused at the door and smiled at him.

Just to cement the experience in her mind. He stepped toward her.

"Yup. Listen, is everything—" he started.

She put a finger on his lips, then took it away and quickly kissed him. "Okay, bye." She let the door swing shut and ran as quietly down the stairs as she could. She didn't want him to think she was running away from him, although she was, and she didn't want Hans to wonder who had been on the roof and come out to check. She hit the alleyway, made sure her car wouldn't be obstructing anything in the morning, and walked briskly around the corner of the block.

She took a shaky, deep breath. Still no shame.

She got to her apartment building a few minutes later, not realizing that she had a wide smile on her face until she caught her reflection in the glass door to the building.

"Well, that escalated quickly," he murmured to himself. Mal had no idea how long he'd been on the roof after she left, looking at the door and looking at the wall he'd just bent her over.

Then the reality set in. He'd fucked the boss's daughter—the one he was supposed to be protecting—and then let her walk home in the middle of the night. *Nice work, you wanker.*

Even then, he didn't make a move to the door. He looked at the roof again, wondering if the whole thing had been some kind of hallucination. Maybe she'd put something in his drink. Or maybe he'd been seduced and abandoned by the one woman he couldn't have.

Didn't want to have.

He ran for the door. He could at least get to his apartment in time to ensure she got home safely. Damn. What had he done? Was he supposed to find her? Try to date her? What did she want?

And why did he care what she wanted? He never had before. Rarely saw a woman more than once, in fact. He always made it clear what the score was, so no one left disappointed. It was a skill, finding a woman who wouldn't be upset by a one-night stand and who wouldn't hold a grudge and let herself into his apartment and burn all his clothes. Because women did that kind of shit, right?

Not to him. Hit and quit, but in a respectful way. He never led them on, never left them anything but happy. He thought of himself as a year-round Santa—spreading only happiness and joy.

Not like Abby. She'd hit and quit him, and it had totally thrown him off balance. What was up with that? By the time he let himself into his apartment, he'd shaken it off. He looked through his camera lens and found her curtains closed as usual and a light on behind them. A shadow suggested she was walking around in there, before it all went dark.

He sighed. At least she'd got home safely, and he hadn't put her in danger. He sat on the bare mattress and dragged his PC toward him.

BARRACKS SECURITY SITREP

Officer: Malone Garrett

Principal: Abigail Baston

Ops Update: She picked up a stranded aid worker from the side of the road last night. Went out to dinner with him. Went home alone. Schedule interrupted. We'll see how her routine plays out tomorrow.

Date of completion: Just waiting for your call.

CHAPTER FIVE

Abby woke up with a warm feeling of calm and relaxation. All stress seemed to have wafted out the open window in her bedroom, like a reverse Peter Pan. She stretched and remembered the previous night. "Malone." She tested the name out as if were an exotic foreign sound. "Malone." She giggled. She'd been so bad, so wanton, and it had been so good. Shame she wouldn't see him again. She wondered what he would be like in a bed, with all the time in the world. Instinctively her fingers fluttered down, pressing against her clit as she recalled the culmination of the previous night.

And then she remembered what day it was. Battery-change day. She sighed. Imagined how changing batteries turned out to be a major day of excitement for her. True, they weren't just any batteries, and true, she'd have to illegally cross an international border to do it, but still. Battery-changing day.

She'd been distracted by the scent of Malone still lingering in her car when she hopped in that morning, and her mind kept flickering back to the previous night—the way he'd spoken to her, the humor in his eyes, then the roof...It wasn't until she'd gotten firm with herself and opened the window to let the eau de Malone go that she got her head back in the game. By the time she arrived at the orphanage, she'd actually figured out a plan to change the batteries without getting caught: It was a wonderful day to play with the kids in the adjacent field. Brigda would be suspicious, but she wouldn't be able to see them.

Under Brigda's disapproving eye, Abby maneuvered all the children into their tiny coats and led them single file into the fields just beyond sight of the farmhouse. They looked adorable all holding hands following one after the other, all bundled up against the crisp morning.

She taught them "I'm a Little Teapot" in English while she turned on the handheld locator that would help her find the ground sensors that needed their batteries changed. The display showed three in the vicinity.

"Keep going," she told the children as they giggled each time they bent over to pour the tea. She had to roll Lana onto her stomach so she could get back on her feet with the bulk of her puffy coat.

Within ten minutes, she'd located and dug for the three ground sensors, then changed their batteries. She'd been told that they lasted for twelve months, but one of her colleagues had warned her before she left for the Ukraine that the cold sometimes made the batteries less effective. It hadn't been that cold since she'd arrived, but she wasn't taking any chances.

The sensors would alert her, and Langley, to anyone crossing the border—which was just a hedge in this part of the country. And then it was her job, and her job alone, to ascertain who had breached the border. Cows, a farmer, or the tanks of the Russian army. And if it was the latter and Abby could officially identify them, then NATO forces would take over. No one wanted World War III, but if it was going to happen, Abby was damned sure it wouldn't be because of an old battery.

With three more to find, she put her bag down and played for a while, letting the children run and jump over her while she was getting her butt wet in the morning dew. Dmitri and Karlov were big enough now to make her "oomph" when they jumped on her, which of course made them want to do it over and over. She laughed, wishing for the simplicity of being a child. Although that wasn't to say these children had had it particularly good in their short lives, but they were luckier than most to have Tanoff and Brigda looking after them.

She lay back with two of the children weaving long, thin reeds through her hair and wondered if Brigda was a threat. Abby had no idea why the woman was so against her being there, except for the perceived threat of having an American so close to the Russian border. But Abby would only be a threat if Brigda ratted her out…

She moved the boys and girls on to the next field, still out of view of the farmhouse, and switched the locator back on. The last three of these sensors abutted the hedge in a V shape. There were still others lining the fields that shared an open border with Russia, but those batteries had been changed when she had first arrived.

After having taught the kids "Oranges and Lemons"—a

rather brutal nursery rhyme that one of her stepmothers had taught her that involved two kids forming an arch while the others tried to walk through fast enough to not get caught as the arch's arms came down at the last line of the song—she went to find the other sensors.

Oranges and lemons, say the bells of St. Clement's.
You owe me five farthings, say the bells of St. Martin's.
When will you pay me? say the bells of Old Bailey.
When I get rich, say the bells of Shoreditch.
When will that be? say the bells of Stepney.
I do not know, says the great bell of Bow.
Here comes a candle to light you to bed. Here comes a chopper to chop off your head!

Mal was sure he was hallucinating and for a split second wondered if the previous night had been a part of it. He hadn't heard that British nursery rhyme since he was five or six, and there was certainly no good reason for him to be hearing it in the Ukrainian countryside, when all the people here were either natives or American. He thought about Hans. Maybe Swiss.

It was a fairly gruesome song—one that could certainly play a big part in some cheap horror movie, and he'd be lying if he said he wasn't slightly spooked by hearing it. Through his binoculars, he could see Abby digging in the field and playing with some kind of handheld machine. Then he caught one of the kids jumping up and down, really just the top of his head, and realized that she must have taken the kids down there too. What was she doing? He couldn't get any closer because she'd see him. But whatever it was, it seemed to have little to do with the orphanage…unless they had some security features out there? Maybe that was it.

He really had no idea. But as long as he had eyes on Abby, he was good. She looked happy today, at least probably the happiest he'd seen her since he started watching her. He wondered if he'd had anything to do with that. His mind had been running over the previous night on and off all day. In all his years, he'd never just shagged a girl—on a roof, no less—and had her disappear with no explanation. He at least asked them out, explored their needs, made sure they weren't looking for a boyfriend or any kind of long-term friendship before closing the deal. He even balked at friends with benefits—he never believed the women who claimed to want that.

His phone vibrated. Baston.

"Garrett here," he said.

"What man did she go to dinner with?" his boss asked with no preamble.

Shit, as soon as he'd woken up, he'd regretted the sitrep he'd sent the night before. He didn't know why he hadn't just sent a same-old, same-old report. He should have seen this coming.

"No one I'd seen before." He flipped onto his back in the grass and closed his eyes and lied through his teeth. "I was with

88

her the whole time. I wouldn't have let anything happen to her."

There was a pause. "Okay, keep me updated. If she sees him again, I want a full background on him. Do you copy?" Baston barked down the phone line.

"Copy that." *She won't see him again.*

His boss hung up. Mal looked at the phone and groaned. Well at least that settled that. He wouldn't be seeing her again, so no need to make up a background investigation.

He rolled back onto his front and aimed his binoculars at Abby again. For a second he couldn't see her, until she came into stark focus—through the lenses she looked as if she were almost on top of him. He pulled his elbows down and lay flat in the grass, hoping she wouldn't see him from the path that led back to the farmhouse.

He held his breath as she walked past him, maybe ten feet from where he was lying. When she passed, he looked up. Her eyes were on the ground, and her hands had children hanging off them. Cute. And then one of the kids turned his head and looked him straight in the eye. He was paralyzed. Why had he looked up? He could have just stayed lying down until she was back inside.

The little boy blinked his light blue eyes at him and grinned a huge, toothless smile and then turned back to keep step with Abby.

He flopped back down. That served him right for trying to cop a look. Jesus. He should have just stuck to the routine. He was here to keep her safe, not discover her every secret. An annoying voice in his head told him that if he knew all her secrets, he'd be better at keeping her safe, but he knew better than to listen to that voice. It had been leading him astray since he'd been fourteen and bunking off school on the streets of London.

He lay in the damp grass again, binoculars held on his chest, and sighed. Was he going to listen to that voice again? Did it have an ulterior motive? Or was he going to value his job and his relationship with his boss—seemingly the only man who could bear to be around him—and leave well enough alone?

The back door to the farmhouse slammed as they went in, and Mal jumped up. From where he stood, he could only see the roof of the house, so it was safe to go back to his car. The wind had suddenly picked up, and the temperature must have dropped at least ten degrees in the hour he'd been in the grass. It was bitter. Tiny flakes of snow drifted past him, and he couldn't believe the abrupt change in weather. He shivered as he got to the car. And then he laughed at himself.

He'd become a right pussy since he left the SAS—the British black-ops special forces that the United States Delta Force was modeled on. While he'd been on the job, he'd lived in a forest in the middle of a snowstorm—for a week. Now *that* had been cold. He'd heated water every day so he could dip his fingers into it to keep them warm enough to operate his weapons. He wondered just how hard-core he still was after the two years of private work he'd done for Baston, since he was honorably discharged after ten years.

Baston knew Mal wasn't easy to like and had an inscrutable past, but one of Mal's old commanders had told him that a bunch of people had quit the SAS to return to the conventional army after Mal had been discharged, just because they didn't fancy their chances going back on a mission without Mal having their back. And that was the only reason Baston had brought him on. And that was the reason, he'd said, that he'd chosen Mal to protect his daughter. He still didn't know if he believed him.

Mal felt a twinge of regret about the previous night and wondered how Baston would feel about Mal if he knew that the only protection he'd shown his daughter so far was a condom. Jesus. What was wrong with him?

He'd never found it hard to stay away from women before; he'd been trained to walk away and not look back. It had always been imperative to the mission to be able to compartmentalize—and that meant never getting attached. But Abby. She was so contrary to appearances. Her life had seemed boring, and she was anything but boring.

Maybe she wouldn't want to see him again anyway, so the mental discussion with himself was moot. To be fair, most normal people—men *and* women—never wanted to see him again. Professionally and privately he fulfilled a need. A specific need that mostly no one wanted to be reminded of afterward. But Abby *wasn't* normal, though.

Or was that his little voice leading him astray again?

CHAPTER SIX

Abby couldn't help slowing down that evening as she passed the bend in the road where she'd picked up Malone the previous night. His car was gone, which meant, she guessed, he'd gotten help and managed to move it. She had wondered, briefly, what she would have done if he was there again, and she'd come to the only right conclusion—drive right past him.

Probably, anyway. It was the right thing to do. The correct CIA field officer procedure for intimate relations: If they were more than casual, they had to be reported. And she'd never, ever had a relationship that she needed to report. She wanted to keep it that way.

Just as she was approaching the outskirts of town, her satellite phone rang. She looked up out of habit to see the stars visible in the sky. The phone they'd given her wasn't exactly top of the line. Unlike in movies and TV shows, they mostly had to make do with any kind of technology that held a reasonable charge. Her satellite phone only really worked when the skies were clear and there wasn't any inclement weather. She'd always been a bit leery of the lack of up-to-date equipment, like the field operatives weren't worth the good stuff.

"This is Baston," she said as she pulled over to the side of the road.

"Hey, chickie," a familiar voice said. It was her partner in crime, Kate. Kate sat on the Russia desk at Langley and kept all the CIA officers up-to-date with intel when she had it. Sometimes her intel had more to do with her own dating life.

"Kate. What's going on?" she asked, smiling to herself.

"I'm dating a Combat Weather guy. I just met him. He told me you had a pocket of clear weather over your location, before the storm cometh, so I thought I'd check in."

"Tell me you didn't reveal my location to your new boyfriend," she said, mock sternly.

"Eh, he has higher clearance than me, so..." Her voice trailed off as she was, no doubt, distracted by something shiny walking past her desk. Abby had witnessed it happen more than once.

"Don't tell me, someone in a sharp uniform just walked by," she deadpanned.

"Man, it's like you're a spy or something." Kate laughed. "Hey, anyway, looks like you have the mother of all storms heading your way, and I wanted to be sure you had everything you needed."

"Sure. I'm okay."

"Look, you haven't been there in the winter. It's hard to keep track of troop movements when the ground is covered in snow and the troops and their carriers are camouflaged in white. Our heat-detecting satellites are pretty crap in sub-Siberia temperatures."

"It defies belief." She and Kate had spoken at length about the shoddy 1980s instruments they had to deal with. Nevertheless, Abby peered through the darkness, feeling excitement spike. "You think we'll see troop movements? What have you heard?"

"Nothing. No need to go to DEFCON 1 or anything. You're just going to be alone and out of range for a while. Keep your eyes open, and stay safe, okay? Check in when you can. Even if it's via email." A couple years back, they'd set up a back-channel protocol in case the encrypted system didn't work or couldn't be accessed. Kate had a slightly different protocol for everyone in the region as a backup. Not terribly legal but also well appreciated when alone in the field with shit tools.

"Copy that," she said.

"And if you have any snowball fights with anyone delicious, I need photos or it didn't happen."

Abby rolled her eyes. "Copy that too." Static crackled over the phone line.

"I'm going to lose you—" Kate said before the phone went dead.

Abby hung up and wondered, not for the first time, if she should just bite the bullet and buy her own freaking sat phone. Not that it would be encrypted and not that the CIA paid her enough to buy one without feeling the pinch financially, but as the clouds rolled in, presumably bringing snow with them, she started to feel a little angry at the shit state of the equipment she had to trust her life to. And at being alone.

It was an argument she'd had with herself many times before. And with Kate. And with her boss.

She started the motor again and made a turn before her street to stock up on food, just in case the snow hit bad. The store was about to close up, but she persuaded the storekeeper to give her five minutes in the aisles. When she'd gathered enough things she could eat with no electricity, she loaded her bags into her car and found a spot to park in the road outside her building. She wondered briefly how her car would hold up in the snow, but with no garage, there wasn't much she could do about it. She swung her bags onto her forearm and locked the door.

A few snowflakes fell on her face, and she looked up to the sky. Having spent some of her childhood in upstate New York, she knew very well that this second, the moment that the snow started, was the prettiest. Silver flakes drifting slowly to earth made her think about her family's first home for a brief second. She breathed in and felt the stir of wind that she knew would bring the snow down in droves.

Suddenly she longed to be inside her apartment, old and creaky as it was, setting her meticulously dried logs and tinder ablaze in her decidedly '70s-inspired fireplace. She scurried down the alleyway to the main entrance to the apartment building.

Mal watched her turn her face up to the sky, and in that second he saw a different side to Abby Baston. Her face lit up as she took in the falling snow, and he wished that he weren't watching through an SLR lens but was standing next to her, maybe brushing the snow from her shoulders.

He sighed. He was kidding himself. He didn't want that. That was what a normal man would want. Not one who travels light and free. Not one who had killed more people than he wished to remember, although remember them he did. Not one who found himself in danger most weeks. Not one who enjoyed the danger he found himself in. But sometimes he liked to pretend he was normal to see how it felt. Like trying on a coat. An awkward, ill-fitting coat.

She passed out of sight, and he waited, eyes on her apartment window for the light to come on. She was on the twenty-second floor, so it mostly depended on how quickly the lift got to her.

He was distracted by two guys walking behind her into the alleyway. One looked behind him as he walked. Mal angled himself to see what he'd been looking at. All he could see from his vantage point were puffs of exhaust coming from a car. An uneasy feeling prickled his skin, and he didn't wait a fraction of a second to act on it.

He grabbed his keys and slammed his door shut behind him. He didn't wait for the lift but ran to the stairwell. Jumping down the stairs four or five at a time and swinging over the railings, he knew he would get to the ground floor faster than waiting for a lift.

He ran across the empty street, getting a good look at the waiting car. It was just one guy looking in his rearview mirror at the entrance to the alleyway. His apprehension kicked up a notch. Barely feeling the cold, even though he was in a thin T-shirt and jeans, he rounded the corner to her apartment complex's entry.

He skidded to a halt. The two men were down. He panted visible puffs of air as he stood over them. Thankfully for the cold, he could also see a tiny waft of air coming from one of them. Not the other. He felt for a pulse. Nada.

Shit. Now what? He found a tin of soup on the ground. Abby had been carrying groceries. Had she killed this guy? Had someone else? Was she upstairs? Had someone taken her? He went into the unmanned lobby. The one lift was ascending. He paused to watch. It stopped at 22. Was she alone now?

Regardless, he couldn't leave these guys here for the police to find. He didn't know what the fuck was going on. He pushed the up button for the lift and pulled out his phone, hitting speed dial number 2.

"Randall Products," a friendly female voice said.

"Three zero zero, please," Mal said.

In less than a second, Randall's voice came over the line. "How can I help?"

"Clean up on aisle three…no four." Dammit, it had been so long since he'd used Randall's services he'd forgotten the protocol.

"Garrett? Is that you?"

"I don't have time—"

"Sure. Address?"

Mal gave him the address of Abby's apartment building.

"It's five k per, and someone will be there in twenty minutes. Can you secure…"

Dammit. "Sure. Give me a second." He shoved his phone into his pants pocket and went back outside. After checking the scene was clear, he took off his T-shirt and grabbed one of the guy's feet, ensuring he didn't leave prints on the man's boots. He dragged him to the far side of a Dumpster and then repeated the process with the other one. He pulled his shirt back on and looked up to see the getaway man standing at the entrance to the alley. *Shit.*

Mal took a step toward him, but the guy whimpered and ran off. Was this just a mugging gone wrong? They certainly didn't seem like hard-core criminals. He remembered Randall and yanked his phone out again. "Look behind the Dumpster for your package," he said. "And what the fuck, man? When did your prices go up to five grand per person?"

"Location, location, location, mate. No one wants to be sent to the gulag."

"Jesus." He wondered if Baston would cover the expense or if it'd have to come out of his savings. Shit, Abby had better be involved somehow or he'd never get his money back. And, yeah, that was cold and he was a-okay with it.

"No worries, mate. Eh. You know I love to double-dip, but someone already called this in. I'll bill them."

"What? Who called it in?"

"Come on, Garrett. Would you want me to tell anyone that you called it in?"

He had a point. Secrecy was the linchpin of his slightly-to-very illegal operation. "Okay. Fair enough," he said, going back into the building. He hit the lift button again.

"How have you been? It's been a long time since I heard from you. Good to hear you're still in the business." Randall had been loosely funded by the dark money in the UK government, and Garrett had often been the sharp end of the dark parts of the government. Their paths had crossed more than once.

"Private now, though," he said. "I've got to go."

"Call me sometime when you don't need something, okay?" Randall said. "Let's catch up."

"Sure." He hung up and got on the lift. They both kind of knew the chance of that happening was remote, but it was good to know he still had an ace in the hole if he needed it.

So who had called in the cleaners already? He was already fighting a suspicion that Abby was in some way mixed up with this. But really there was no evidence that she'd been there at all. Except the soup. Maybe she'd already been on the lift when all that went down. Maybe they tried to mug some guy and he fought back.

There was only one way to find out. He stepped out on the twenty-second floor and paused. A half-wrecked plastic grocery bag full of food was strewn across the landing in front of her door. Shit. Was someone in there with her? Had the fight extended to her apartment?

Before he'd even finished the thought, he kicked in her door. It was dark. He took one step—actually barely even a suggestion of a step—and a big frying pan swung at his face.

He ducked and swiveled, kicking the legs out from under his assailant.

Whoever it was fell but scrambled away. He grabbed the leg nearest him and pulled. It kicked back in his face until he let them go. He sprung up and hit the lights. No more fighting in the dark. What the fuck?

It was Abby.

CHAPTER SEVEN

Abby, wait. It's just me," he said, holding up his hands as if in surrender.

Her eyes blazed as she dipped her head and ran full tilt. She slammed into him and he went sprawling. She landed on top of him, and as his head slammed into the doorjamb, he saw stars around the periphery of his vision. He fought to stay conscious.

Abby jumped off him and reached for the frying pan again. He wanted to shake her. Couldn't she see it was him? Had she been blinded by the sudden light?

He tried to grab for her leg but missed. Dammit. Shaking his head to clear his vision, he got to his feet, the sudden altitude bringing everything thankfully into sharp relief again.

"Abby. Stop!" He tried again to make her actually look at him. She peered up at him for a second from the floor.

She'd reached the damned frying pan.

"Nope," was all she said before she spun her legs around so her feet were pointing away from him and sprang up. As she did, she swung the pan upward with such force that it would certainly have broken his jaw if he hadn't bent away from the swing.

Jesus, there was no way she was an orphanage worker. As far as he knew, Aide Internationale didn't have a combat unit.

"What's the matter with you? Fucking stop, will you?" he said again.

Her eyes darted around in an exercise he knew well. She was looking for another weapon. No way.

He grabbed her in a bear hug from behind, pinning her arms to her sides. "Okay, now you're listening—" he began.

She dipped her head and reverse head butted him. Pain spread through his face. He'd pulled his head away enough that it hadn't broken his nose, but now he was fucking pissed off.

He still had her in his grip, so he pushed her away, over the back of her sofa. She expelled air as she bounced over the cushions onto the floor, hitting her shoulder on her coffee table.

"Can you just stop now? I don't want to hurt you," he said, rubbing the side of his face. Jesus, he wasn't sure her father was paying him enough.

"Well that makes one of us," she said, running to the kitchen.

Oh shit. She was going to eggbeater him to death. Or knife him. Neither was that appealing. Seriously, if she emerged with a knife, that was it. Fucking boss's daughter or fucking not.

No sense in following her into the room that was so small there was a chance he could actually stumble onto a knife accidentally.

She came out wielding a knife, of course. Typical. "Well come on, then, get it over with. Stop fucking dancing around like you think I might just leave. I'm not leaving." Why, though, he didn't know. He could just leave and resume following her from afar. And to think, he'd only come up to make sure she was okay. He sighed. "Come on. Give it your best shot, little girl."

As he suspected, his last words galvanized her. Anger flashed across her face.

Satisfaction came over him. Anger made people sloppy. He grinned and tilted his head, mocking her.

She leapt at him, knife poised to slash him. He shifted balance at the last moment, using his hands to push her away. She stumbled into the wall behind him but regrouped fast enough to slash at his arm. He looked down in disbelief and concern. She really did want to hurt him. And if he let her get close enough, he was going to have to put her down.

He stepped away from her. "Okay. You've made your intentions perfectly clear. You think you want to hurt me, and if I stand perfectly still and don't defend myself, you probably can. But, and I can't emphasize this enough, if you come at me again, I will hurt you. I don't want to hurt you, but I don't want you to kill me for some half-baked, ill-thought-out reason. Do you understand me?"

She approached him again, moving the knife across her body, like a pro, waiting for the ideal place to strike. She took it.

Mal stepped away from it and punched her knife-carrying arm hard enough to make her fingers lose sensation. It worked. Her face fell as her arm dropped uselessly to her side, the knife clattering to the tile floor. "I'm sorry about that, but you need to just calm the fuck down for a minute."

He did nothing other than blink, his guard down for a second, before she suddenly had another knife in her other hand. She pushed him against the wall and held the knife to his throat. What the fuck just happened?

He wasn't scared. He could still kill her with his bare hands if he wanted to. This was nothing more than a slightly rough dance to him, but he begrudgingly admitted that she had some skills too. And there was a much higher possibility that it was she who had hurt and maybe killed the two men outside.

Her eyes blazed not three inches from his. If he hadn't been a little curious about who Baston's daughter was—indeed, if she even was Baston's daughter—he would have been turned on by the fury she showed. By her physicality and her strength.

She pressed the knife to his throat, not easing up the pressure even when he felt the warm trickle of blood down his neck. Shit. She was sexy, and violent.

He leaned toward her mouth, suddenly wanting to kiss her more than he wanted the knife away from his jugular. The knife held constant, but he didn't. Even though she didn't let up pressure for one second, in that second he valued the kiss more than the knife.

She startled when his lips touched hers, jerking away, and then back to his. He was kissing a woman who was holding a knife to his throat. Fuck, it was sexy.

She was lost for a second. And in that second she forgot she was holding a knife. Forgot that she was slicing into the neck of the man she'd had sex with the previous night. Forgot that he was an unknown player in the fight she'd just had with two guys she'd never seen before.

His mouth pressed against hers, sending a jolt of awareness through her. The fight that had left her bruised and a little bloody had injected a mother lode of adrenaline rushing her veins like a burst dam. Even though she'd just beaten two men, she'd never felt more like a woman. A powerful woman.

Kissing a jerk who... Yeah, who what?

She jerked away from him, slamming his head back into the wall with her palm on his forehead.

"Who the fuck are you?" she said in a low voice. Last thing she needed was her neighbors poking their heads into her apartment.

"Malone Garrett," he replied through his teeth.

"How do you know where I live? How do you know the men outside?" As she asked the questions, she realized that his car trouble had been a setup. He'd known she'd pick him up. She hated that he'd predicted her actions. And then had sex with her.

She ignored the voice in her head that told her it was she who had instigated their rooftop liaison. Had he predicted that too?

Her knife pressed harder against his throat. "You have five seconds before I slice."

He waited until she'd mentally reached five before opening his mouth. "I live across the road. I saw you come home, from my window." He shrugged. "I was going to come and ask you out again, but..."

"Nope. Not even close." Suddenly she had total courage of her convictions. She'd just annihilated two men who had threatened her, and she knew she was right about him.

"You've been following me. You set yourself up at the side of the road so I'd pick you up, right?"

"No. My car had broken down. I—"

"What was wrong with it?" she asked.

He hesitated. A long, silent second.

Just as she thought. "Exactly. Who are you, and why are you following me? I'm not afraid to kill you. I'm not afraid of anything." Except maybe the Russians. And Brigda a little.

Mal rolled his eyes and calmly found her thumb with his hand and bent it back until it popped. The knife dropped to the ground again.

"Shit. You bastard." She backed away from him, holding her hand in pain. Goddamn him. He took a step toward her and with no other choice, she popped her thumb back in its socket. She nearly threw up, but in the haze of pain, she managed to put the sofa between them.

He didn't make a move on her, just grabbed some tissues

from her flowery Kleenex box holder and held them to his neck. They instantly flashed red with the blood flowing from his wound.

She turned away from him for a split second, reaching for the weapon under the armchair seat cushion. When she turned back with the gun pointed at his head, she was startled to see his cell phone at his ear.

"Yup. Put me through to Baston, please."

What?

He raised his eyebrows at her and smiled an innocent smile.

"No, n-no, wait...," she stuttered, trying to get her head around the fact that this obtuse British man knew her father.

"What?" He held his finger up at her for a second. "Yup. I'll hold." He listened for a second and then pulled the phone an inch from his ear. "I'm guessing you have about three more bars of 'Greensleeves' to put that gun the fuck down and stop rampaging, or I'll tell your father that you have me at gunpoint and that you are quite clearly not an Aide Internationale worker."

Shit. He couldn't know. No one could know. She had a vision of her ordered life and structured relationships with her family crumbling under this information.

She held the gun and her other hand up. "Okay, okay. Hang up."

"Put the gun down first," he said, jamming the phone back to his ear.

"Okay. It's down." She threw it onto the sofa.

He picked it up and checked the safety, then pulled the

magazine out, pushing the top round down to check it. It was full. She'd never fired it. Then he put the phone back in his pocket without hanging up. Shit. She'd been fooled by the oldest trick in the book.

"You weren't calling my father?" she asked, sinking to the now weaponless sofa.

"Nope. I don't like to report in until I have a full picture. So let's talk and you can tell me what the fuck you're doing here, and with luck, this whole little family tale will have me back home before the week's out." He sat on the sofa arm and gestured at her with the gun. "Come on, sweetheart. Spill your guts."

God, she hated him. He looked so cocky, so sure of himself. So unconcerned. Well, fuck that. "I'm not telling you anything until you tell me what you're doing here." She suspected that her father had sent him to watch her. Anger pulsed in her like an infection. She was too old to be treated like a child.

"I think you know what I'm doing here. I have the shittiest job in the world. I've spent the best part of this year in war zones. Killing bad people, rescuing good. Sometimes getting good guys killed. Protecting people, sometimes protecting bad people. And for the last couple of weeks I've had the most boring job in the world: watching a woman with the dullest life, who obviously doesn't need my protection. And let me tell you this. It was worth my sliced and diced neck just to get off this fucking job. I'm going to tell your father that you don't need my help, and I will be out of here." He cocked his head and looked out the window. "Somewhere warm. Somewhere I can get drinks without vodka in them. Somewhere the women are in bikinis, not full-body sheepskin." He looked at her coat on its hook. "It's not an attractive look, you know."

So he was a dick as well. Not the smooth, suave, handsome man she'd met the night before. That had been an act. She made a face. She'd had sex with him.

"Yeah, I know. I've been pulling that face when I think about last night too," he said, as if he were discussing the weather. He shrugged. "For me it's an occupational hazard. Not sure what it was for you, though." He grinned.

"Pretty horrible. Desperation. It was you or Hans, and he couldn't leave the restaurant until much later. I wanted to get to bed early. I could tell you'd be quick." She gave him a fake sympathetic smile and cocked her head. "You know they have drugs for that kind of…problem now, don't you?"

His eyes narrowed. Strike.

"Tell me who you are, and what you're doing here," he said.

She tucked her legs under her as if she were having a chat with a girlfriend. "You go first."

"I'm the one with the phone and the gun. And the temper. You go first."

She was strictly not allowed to tell anyone she was a CIA field operative. Not her family, and certainly not random people whom she happened to have sex with. Or people who hold her at gunpoint. "I've got nothing to tell you."

In the silence that fell between them, a tone sounded. A beep. A loud and insistent bleeping. For a second she had no idea what it was. Was it something he had on him? No, not judging by his frown. Her eyes traced the room and alighted on the shopping and her handbag still on the floor. Her phone never bleeped like that.

Oh. Holy motherfucking shit. She knew exactly what it was. Her eyes met his, which she knew did not reflect the horror in hers. She was going to have to come clean.

Emergency measures.

And she needed him. Maybe.

CHAPTER EIGHT

She was a bitch as well as a complete waste of time. How could Baston—your everyday good guy—give him this job? The worst job Mal had been assigned since he started at Barracks Security. And that included being shot at, being interrogated by a warlord in Afghanistan, and suffering through fellow operatives inexplicably falling in love. He'd rather be back in the cave in Taliban-controlled Helmand Province than watch good guys make fools of themselves again. Over women. Jesus.

And if she didn't turn that fucking beeping off, he would stamp on every piece of electronics in the house. "Whatever that is, turn it off before I shoot it."

Her superior expression had vanished, leaving a wan face with alarmed eyes. He sighed. "Jesus, tell me it's not a bomb."

She swallowed and nodded to her bag. "Worse."

What could be worse than a bomb? "Start talking, sweetheart."

She took a deep breath and looked as if she was about to say everything. Instead she lunged for her bag. He stood up and leveled his gun at her again, but she ignored him.

She straightened with a black remote control thing. "Shit."

"What is that?" he asked, determined not to drop his aim even though he realized that he wasn't going to shoot his boss's daughter under any circumstances. You know, unless she *really* pissed him off.

"World War Three. Maybe." She shrugged, but fear flickered across her face and took up residence in her eyes.

He lowered the gun. "I can't help you if you don't tell me."

"What are you going to tell my father?" she hedged.

His patience evaporated. "Whatever I damn well please, you psycho. That you're a trained killer, that you disabled two muggers downstairs, that you sliced my neck open. Hell, maybe I'll just call the police and let them have you."

"The police?" She looked at her watch. "There's no evidence left now. They'll probably arrest *you*." Her triumphant smirk made him want to kill her, or put his fist through something. Anything.

She was right. Randall's people would have worked their magic by now.

"Okay, so Daddy it is." He tucked his gun into his waistband and reached for his phone.

"You probably don't want to do that. I'd get you fired in a heartbeat," she said, almost absentmindedly looking at the amber flashing light on the remote control. The beeping had thankfully stopped.

"Oh yeah? And how are you going to do that?"

She cast her eyes to the ground for a few seconds. When she looked at him, tears were running down her face. He made a step toward her. What just happened? But she stretched her thumb and pinky finger out to make a finger phone, held it to her ear, and said, "Daddy…that man?" she sobbed realistically. "That man you sent? He…he seduced me and then…and then he left me"—more sobs—"saying that he'd only screwed me to screw you…" She cocked her head, tears drying instantly, and slammed her imaginary phone down. "Get it?"

Wow. "Dude. What's the matter with you?" he said. "Your daddy issues are out of control. Do you want to talk about it? I understand they have therapy for things like that now." He couldn't resist getting her back for her earlier implication about his endurance.

"Just get out."

He laughed. "No fucking way, sweetheart. I don't know who you are, or what you're doing here, but neither of us is getting out of this building tonight." He glanced through the window at the whiteout in the street. "You're just going to have to tell me what's going on or suffer the consequences." He cracked his knuckles, even though he had no idea what the consequences would be. He dropped his voice into what he hoped was a soothing tone. "Just tell me what's going on, and I'll see if I can help." He shrugged and sat on the sofa, patting the spot next to him. Ah. A condescending note too far, obviously, when she sat on the armchair under which her gun had been stashed.

He knuckles were white around the remote control she was holding.

"Let's start with that," he said, nodding toward her hands. "What is it?"

She sighed. "It's a ground sensor."

He waited for more information; none seemed to be coming. He sighed and leaned back on the sofa, ready for a long haul of questions.

"What does it sense? Water? Radiation? Earthquakes?" he asked calmly.

"Movement," she said, still perched at the edge of the chair.

He hoped it wasn't alerting her to the fact that he'd put a movement sensor under the carpet in front of her door. That couldn't be it.

"Where is it alerting you to movement?"

She raised an eyebrow and held up the remote. "Here?"

"Don't be such a bloody child. If you want my help—"

"When did I ever say I needed or wanted your help? You're nothing but a momentary distraction. Something I have to deal with before I can get to work. I don't even know what you're doing here, and frankly I don't care."

And then everything went dark.

Awesome. Just fucking awesome. She took a deep, steadying breath. "You really think the roads are impassable now?" she asked, trying to eke out a plan from her tired brain.

His voice was calm. "We could get out on foot but not

in a vehicle. Unless you have a snow machine in your bedroom."

"I knew there was something I forgot to order...," she said weakly.

He did her the honor of not forcing a laugh at her lame joke.

The darkness pervaded throughout the room. With no light outside, not by the moon nor streetlights, her eyes could only barely make out his silhouette across the room from her. He hadn't moved, still sitting motionless on the arm of the sofa. She had to tell him what she was doing there.

She'd been at the CIA for nearly ten years, recruited before she'd completed her first semester at college. She'd told no one. She just hadn't felt close enough to her older brothers, nor to her father. Although he was another problem entirely.

But in all her years, the one thing that had been beaten into her brain day after day, month after month, was service before self. She might be worried about losing her job for telling him what she was doing there, but if she didn't, she would certainly not complete her mission.

Mission before everything.

"I don't work for Aide Internationale," she said.

"No fucking kidding," he said, getting up off the arm and resettling on the sofa. Obviously he had the idea that this was going to be a long story. But it wasn't.

"Well, I do actually work for Aide Internationale. They pay me, but I'm CIA. I'm here to keep watch on the border. The Russian analysts at Langley think that all the Russian posturing at the G20 meetings was a distraction for them invading Ukraine."

He was silent for a few beats. "I was there. For the G20 shenanigans."

She didn't really want to think about that. "Anyway, this sensor was placed by my predecessor. These ones are placed ten klicks inside the border on the Russian side."

"He had balls of steel on him to do that," Malone said.

"Yes, *she* did." Abby couldn't help smiling as she said it. She had some big shoes to fill.

"So what makes you think a farm tractor didn't trigger it? Or a malfunction?" he asked in the darkness.

"Who uses a tractor in the middle of the night in a snowstorm?" As she said it, she realized that it was possible. A stranded animal in a snowstorm? A tractor might be the only way to get to it.

"How many sensors do you have?" he asked.

"I can't tell you that," she said. There were thirty along the border ten kilometers inside the Russian border and another ten or so in the acres behind the orphanage. The theory being that they wouldn't want to cross the border on roads where they would be seen, filmed on some kid's cell phone, and posted on YouTube, with CNN reporters on the ground before they'd stopped for a bathroom break. And with NATO bombs before lunch. The common theory was that they'd use the farmlands to enter the northeastern part of Ukraine. They already had the Crimea. The Russian president wanted the rest. And God only knew where he would stop.

"How will you know the difference between those 'pro-Russian fighters' and the real Russian army?"

She hated that he knew all the right questions to ask. "You're assuming that the 'pro-Russian fighters' aren't the Russian army, and I think they are. I just have to be there to prove it. An insignia, a unit with military-issue weapons, uniforms, recognizable military vehicles that we can compare with those bought by the Russian government. That's what I'm here for. If I can show that they are the Russian army, then the might of the NATO forces will rain down on them before they get to any densely inhabited areas." She wanted to be there to see that so badly.

He was silent, barely moving at all. Maybe the dark had made it easier to talk, to basically spill all the secrets she'd held in for so long. She sighed. Maybe he wasn't such a dick after all.

As soon as the thought formed in her brain, he jumped up. "Excellent. Well, it seems like you've got it all under control, and that means I can tell your father you don't need any further protection and I can get reassigned. Somewhere less dangerous than your apartment. Like Kabul."

She sprang up too. "No. You can't tell my father. So you're stuck here. Or I'll have you arrested."

"What are you talking about? Of course you can tell your father." He checked the safety on the gun. "I'm going to keep this, by the way. It's the penance you pay for pointing it at me."

"Wait." She put herself between him and the door. "My father does jobs for foreign governments, private corporations based who-knows-where. So I can't tell him without losing my clearance and my job. If you tell him, you'll be arrested. And fired." She got as far as pulling a sad face and bringing her fingers up to her face again, mimicking a phone, before he grabbed her hand.

"Okay, enough." He dragged his hand through his hair and sighed. "Jesus. How did this happen? Suddenly watching you from across the street feels like a dream. *Fuck*."

"You were watching me? All the time?" she asked, a cold finger of creepiness poking her in the place were butterflies usually lived.

"Enough to know you can set soup on fire and inexplicably spill it down your…" He nodded to her breasts. "Not sure how you managed that."

"I was startled by a mouse in the kitchen. A big mouse. Anyone would have jumped." She put her fists on her hips.

"You have mice in here?"

She shrugged. "Just one. Boris." As the words formed, she realized how ridiculous it made her sound.

"You named the mouse?"

"Jesus. Russians could be encroaching on the Ukrainian border, World War freaking Three could start tomorrow, and you're making fun of me? Fine. I decided that instead of being freaked out by it, I'd make him a pet. That way it wasn't so awful thinking he was around. Besides, I'm beginning to realize that he's better company than you are."

He ignored the last part. "Why didn't you just shoot it?"

"I was saving all my rounds for you." God, he was annoying. She wondered if he was one of those guys who figured everything a woman did was "the wrong way" or just wrong. She wished they could go back to fighting. That felt more real and honest than this verbal smackdown.

"Well to be fair, who knows what you might have ended up shooting." He shrugged and went back to the window, peering out into the thick snowfall.

She fisted her hands, wanting to just punch him. A lot. She wished she had a punching bag with her. "Is it possible that you could stop being a dick for a moment?"

His eyes remained on the street. "Doubtful. That's my default."

"How is it possible that you have friends?" she said, needing a drink.

"I try not to. Too complicated," he murmured.

She got some shot glasses and grabbed her bottle of contraband Grey Goose. She shoved the glass at him, making him turn around. "You know, you'd have to be fairly simpleminded to think that having friends was complicated. What else do you find complicated? Uno? Tic-tac-toe?"

"I don't know what either of those things are," he said, taking the shot glass. "You don't have anything other than vodka?"

"Sure. Maybe Malibu would be more your thing?" she said, pouring a double shot for herself.

Malone gave her a pissed stare and held his glass out to be filled. She did.

Abby wasn't sure why she kept sniping at him, except it was fun and exercised a part of her brain that had been dormant for six months. It was difficult to banter with people when you didn't speak their language fluently.

But she was also relieved he hadn't left. She didn't need his help, but she wanted it. He was obviously skilled; otherwise her father wouldn't have employed him or put him within a mile of his daughter.

She had no satellite communications and no secure way of contacting anyone without the call being tracked and traced. She'd already risked too much by calling Randall from her burner phone, which she'd then destroyed and thrown into the Dumpster next to the guys who had attacked her. Now she had no means of communicating with anyone until the power came back on. She felt impotent. Damn the snow. Damn those guys. She sat on the sofa, putting the vodka bottle on the coffee table.

"Who were they?" Malone asked, sitting beside her, yet a decent distance away. He tipped more vodka into his glass and leaned back.

"Who?"

"They men who attacked you."

"Oh, them. I don't know. I've never seen them before. Probably muggers." She was proud that she'd neutralized them so easily. "They definitely weren't professionals. More like opportunists. Snow, no one on the streets, and then they happen across a lone woman with her hands full and her purse easily accessible." She shrugged and took another sip from her glass.

"Then how do you know Randall?" he asked.

She cocked her head. "Who?" She was just buying time here, and frankly she wasn't sure why. He already knew too much to let him walk off.

He looked meaningfully at her but said nothing.

Oh hell. "My analyst gave me his contact number in case of emergencies. I didn't want them to regain consciousness and then come find me. I couldn't call the police because how would I explain? That I took karate as a kid?" She downed the rest of the vodka and leaned forward to pour more, holding it for him to offer his glass. "So are you going to stick around for a bit? Maybe help stop the next all-out ground war?"

CHAPTER NINE

She didn't realize that she'd killed one of the men. There was a part of him that knew he should tell her—to prepare her should the authorities get involved. But another, bigger, part wanted to keep that knowledge from her.

He didn't know her. Maybe she'd killed many people, but he didn't think so. Behind her brassy ballsiness lay an operative who, he thought, might not be fine with the fact that she'd killed someone. There was no harm in not telling her for now.

"Well, when you put it like that," he said, "I guess it would be rude not to."

"We need to get out to the site as soon as possible," she said, looking anxiously out the window.

"Not while it's snowing. It's too unpredictable. I've known fully trained"—he wanted to say SAS operatives, but he wasn't going to volunteer his résumé unless she asked specifically—"men get disoriented and severely frostbitten in snowstorms. The rule is, you move when it stops."

"As soon as it stops," she said. "It's still early. Around seven?" Her eyes searched for the wall clock that was invisible in the darkness.

He clicked his watch. "It's five past nine. Get some rest—I'll take the first shift. In two hours, I'll wake you up." He turned back to the window and leaned against the frame, looking out into the white oblivion, not wanting to see her struggle with him taking control and wondering how he could get them all the way back to the orphanage without dying.

"Okay," she said eventually. He heard her stomp off to the bedroom and close the door behind her. Under normal circumstances, he would follow her, convince her that it would be best if they stayed awake together and did something to pass the time. But for some reason, he found the idea of such a manipulation unsavory. Probably because too much depended on them working together. He snorted a quiet laugh. He still hadn't entirely bought into her deductions about the sensors and the Russian invasion.

The snow had stopped swirling like an image on a Christmas card and was now coming down at an angle, reflecting just how hard the wind was blowing. One thing he was sure of: If she was going to drag him out into snowmageddon, he'd better get his winter gear from his place.

His apartment was cold and dark—unsurprisingly since he'd done no insulating with rugs or furniture. He stopped to put his computer equipment in a gap beneath the floorboards that he'd made the first week he'd been there.

As he collected his kit bag, he looked around the room again. For an uneasy moment he wondered if he was looking at his life. Barren of comfort, cold and dark. Then he shrugged. Better that than cluttered and messy. Probably.

By the time he returned to Abby's apartment, he'd been gone maybe twenty minutes. He opened the door quietly but stopped when he heard her calling his name in a whisper. Was someone else in there with her? Was she trying to get his attention so he could help her? He stepped in, quietly closed the door, and dropped his snow gear silently to the floor. He took the gun from his waistband and peered into the darkness.

"Malone? Garrett?" her voice came again. Was that a note of panic he heard? Was she crying? Dammit, why hadn't he paid more attention to the way women sounded when he upset them? Then she came out of the kitchen, her chest heaving beneath a kind of long, thin, misbuttoned cardigan. Her legs and feet were bare.

"What is it?" he whispered, even though he didn't know why.

She jumped and stared at him, panic draining from her eyes. Then she dropped her eyes to the ground and took some deep breaths. "Nothing. I just needed a drink."

No, she didn't. She'd thought he'd left her. She'd gone looking for him and hadn't found him and panicked. For all her tough talk..."It's okay. I'm here," he said in a soft voice, putting his gun on the table and advancing on her.

Her voice became more certain. "I don't care. I was looking for a drink."

"Sure you were, sweetheart. A drink called 'Malone? Garrett?'" He raised an eyebrow at her, trying to provoke the fear out of her by mimicking her. He was still closing the gap between them slowly, as if trying not to startle a scared animal.

She clocked his move before he'd got within arm's reach. She started backing away from him.

She cleared her throat. "I was just making sure you weren't out here. I didn't want you seeing me with barely anything on."

"Yeah, you were terrified of that yesterday." He shook his head. If he'd choreographed this right, she would get mad again and regain her courage.

He didn't stop advancing, even though he could see she was about to find the kitchen wall at her back.

She found it. He stopped inches away from her.

"Just because I wanted you to see me naked yesterday doesn't mean I want you to see me naked today." She put her hands on her hips.

It worked. She overcame whatever crisis he'd walked in on, and now she was back to her annoying self. "Very true." He stepped away so that she knew he wasn't a threat, but as soon as he'd taken a step back, she grabbed the front of his shirt, screwed it up into her fist, and yanked him toward her. Heat rushed through him as her lips met his. *Alrighty then.*

"You...are the most...annoying person...I've ever...met," she said, punctuating her words with kisses.

"Pot, meet the kettle," he murmured back. The wafer-thin cardigan she was wearing was driving him insane. He could feel the heat of her skin, but the material was slightly rough. Rougher than her skin anyway. He pushed her back against the wall and took a breath. He was being a wanker again. Fucking the boss's daughter like it was okay.

It wasn't okay.

"Are you sure you're…"

"Jesus, spare me the bleeding heart, Malone. I want what I want. Right now, I want you. If you're up for it, do something. If you're not—"

He licked the whole length of his palm slowly, cutting off her words as she watched his tongue. Then he plunged his hand in her panties and dragged his fingers through her wetness, making her gasp and hold on to the wall like it would hold her up.

He used all his fingers to stroke different parts of her. "Does this 'something' work for you, love?" he growled, pressure building in his pants.

She moaned in response, the sound reverberating through his soul. *Jesus.*

He took his hand away and slung her over his shoulder.

"What are you doing?" she gasped as he strode toward her bedroom.

"I'm not going to fuck you against a wall again, sweetheart. That might work for you…"

"It does work for me," she said, he voice coming out in time with his strides.

"I know." He opened the door and lowered her gently to the floor.

Immediately her fists went to her hips again. He was too turned on to argue, so he just pushed her back. She fell onto the bed with a small squeal.

"You might want to get screwed against a wall, but if I'm…*servicing* you, you're going to fucking look at me. You're going to see me making you come. I'm not an anonymous dick." He had zero fucking idea why he was suddenly so passionately against anonymous sex. But apparently he was.

He stood at the foot of the bed. "Strip," he said.

She hesitated.

"Get your fucking clothes off."

When she'd gone looking for him because she couldn't sleep, she'd imagined they could look at maps and make a plan for when the snow stopped. But when she'd found him gone, she slipped into an unfamiliar state of fear and trepidation. He'd left her.

Suddenly she'd had doubts that she would be able to get to the border by herself in the drifting snow before the Russians or, yes, maybe a guy on a tractor. This was her job. As soon as she'd realized that maybe she wouldn't have to do it herself, that maybe he'd be able to help her, she'd subconsciously decided that she *couldn't* do it by herself.

What was wrong *with her?*

And while her body was flooding with stage one hysteria, he'd come back. And thirty seconds later she was here, standing on her bed—a bed that had seen no action in over six months—deliberating whether to do a silent striptease.

Who knew when she'd get laid again? Who knew when she'd meet a sufficiently hot man who was also annoying enough that she wouldn't want to get close to him?

"Take them off, or I'll take them off for you," he said in a challenging voice.

"You can try…," she said, and readied herself for combat.

But he didn't grab her, didn't jump on her and rip off her

clothes. Unexpectedly, he stood up on the bed with her, taking her hand to steady them on the bouncy mattress. He brushed hair out of her eyes and kissed her. Deeply, slowly, like he was truly in love with her. An unrecognizable emotion crested over her, sending waves of warmth pulsing through her body in time with every touch of his tongue.

Her muscles loosened as the kiss continued. One of his hands pulled her hair back, like he'd done the previous night, but gently, insistently, until she presented her throat to him. He kissed down her neck; the chill of the air in the room fanned over the moisture he left on her skin. She shivered.

He rubbed his hands up and down her arms, as if to warm her. She let him wrap his body around her. She couldn't tell if his proximity was making her light-headed or if the mattress was definitely not solid ground.

In one slick movement, he pulled her cardigan from the bottom and drew it slowly up her body. Goose bumps followed his hand as her skin was introduced to the night air. He pulled it over her head, the material scratching her nipples in an almost unbearable way.

As the garment hit the floor, the air—so cold around her—rendered her skin impossibly taut and tender. She expected him to ravish her, but no, still so much restraint. She didn't know if she liked him this way—it felt personal, as if he were establishing a connection with something inside of her. Except she knew he wasn't that type. He didn't seem to be that type.

He held her gaze as he swept a foot out and took hers out

from under her. She fell on the bed, a half gasp, half laugh escaping as she bounced. He wasn't that type.

"Oldest trick in the book, babe," he said, pulling off his own shirt. He jumped off the bed effortlessly and undid his pants, pushing them down so he could step out of them.

All she could see was his erection. "You're the oldest trick in the book." She grinned as she held a hand out to him.

He ignored her hand and sat next to her. She propped herself up on her elbows.

"You're fearless," he said, running a hand over her stomach.

Clearly he hadn't registered her near panic when she'd thought he'd left her—and her country—high and dry. "No one's fearless. It's too dangerous," she said.

"I don't mean on the job. I mean here. With me. You barely know me, and you're not embarrassed, or scared, or anxious about me being here, seeing you naked when most people feel the most vulnerable."

She frowned. "I don't feel vulnerable. Should I?"

"Most women would," he replied, running his index finger lightly around her nipple.

"I'm not most women," she said, almost arching into his touch.

"You're not. You've been trained."

She knew what he meant. He'd clearly been through the same training. Do what you have to do to protect your country's interests. Decide how far you're prepared to go. Know you can handle yourself if things go wrong. Give your body if you have to but not your emotions, not your thoughts, definitely not your love.

"As have you. You know who trained me. Who trained you?" She wondered if he was MI6, or maybe MI5 before he'd joined her father's outfit.

He paused, his eyes searching hers. "The Regiment," he said simply.

She forced herself not to react. "The Regiment" was insider code for SAS, the British Special Air Service. The black-ops unit so hard-core that she'd heard that people died just trying out to attend their training course. She was elated that she had someone so qualified to help her, and concerned too. What if she was being played? She knew people in black-ops divisions often had questionable morals and bendable ethics.

"I don't know if I'm scared or turned on," she said honestly.

"You should be both, love. I was in for a long time." He stroked her gently through her panties.

She wanted to question him further. In fact, she had a duty to her country to find out what she could about him, but it wasn't that that was driving her curiosity. It was a desire to know him. And she had to fucking squelch that feeling immediately. She grabbed his hand and held it against her panties. She held his gaze. "I want to talk about that. But not now. Right now I don't want to talk about anything. I don't want to think about anything. I just want you."

"I think it's sweet that you think I'd tell you anything about my previous job, but I take your point." He wasted no time in getting rid of her panties. Instead of lying beside her, he yanked her legs open and knelt between them.

She sank back to the pillows. *Yes!*

His tongue wasn't shy. She felt its hard stroke through her

whole body. He pulled her legs farther apart and slipped his fingers through her folds to her wetness. The heat of his tongue and the cool of his harder fingers sent her whole world into a tailspin. Her fingers tangled in the bedcovers as the tip of his tongue probed her. God, she needed this. This utter release from rational thought, rational feeling.

Heat zipped through her body, not just from his mouth and hands, but also from the feeling that she was opening herself to him without having to talk. Without having to actually open herself mentally. It was bliss. She shut off thoughts of Russia, thoughts of the SAS, and thoughts of her CIA masters frothing at the bit because she was alone in a snowstorm.

Wave after wave of freedom and heat and desire washed over her—her conflicting thoughts and emotions fading away in an ocean of need.

He slipped a finger inside her, and she bucked against him. As his tongue assaulted her clitoris, she gasped and struggled to let herself go. The sensation drove her insane. Heat accumulated in her shoulders, flashing through her as if she were attached to an electrical outlet. His hands and tongue worked magic. His fingers curled inside of her, triggering tremors throughout her body, and his tongue circled her clit until her breaths came in pants, and then gasps as she urged the wave of orgasm to crash over her. It did, taking rational thought and feeling with it as her body arched from the bed almost as if it thought it would make the sensation last longer.

Ragged breaths came from her as she urged him up. She opened her eyes to find him fishing for a condom from his pants pocket. She allowed herself a little smile. She loved a responsible, well-prepared man. When his eyes rested on hers, though, he didn't smile back.

"You're a bloody terrible person, you know?" he said as he took his dick in his hand.

She blinked. "What do you mean?"

"Threatening to tell your father I seduced and abandoned you." With one thrust he was deep inside her, taking any protest from her lips. But he wouldn't stop talking.

"Using me on the rooftop," he whispered as he started moving, causing the most beautiful friction between their bodies.

"Blackmailing me. Pulling a gun on me."

"Mmm-hmm," was all she could say as she arched into a thrust that seemed to touch her whole body.

"Slicing my neck."

But revenge would be hers. She took a breath and opened her eyes. "Stop." She put her hands on his hips to stop his movement.

He froze. "What's wrong?" His brow furrowed in concern. Sucker.

She took advantage of his bewilderment and slipped a thigh between his. It took all her strength to flip him. It wasn't elegant, but it surprised the crap out of him.

"What the…?"

She straddled him and held his dick to her. "You're a bloody terrible person, you know," she said, mimicking an English accent. She slid him into her in one smooth stroke, making him groan.

"You followed me for days." She raised and hesitated before lowering onto him again.

He strained to be inside her.

She slid back down. "You took photos of me, without me knowing." She dug her nails into his hips, feeling what *had* been manufactured outrage turning into real anger. "You pretended to be someone else. And then you fucked me."

"I don't remember you complaining about any of that," he ground out between gritted teeth.

"I am now," she snarled back. Fury drove her. How dare he treat her like someone to be used? Blackmail was the perfect response for a man like him. The fire in her belly met her arousal in a battle to the death.

He splayed his hands over her breasts, pulling her nipples between his fingers as she rode him. The twin sensations joined the anger and desire in a rush of lightning inside her. Her orgasm rose sharply, without warning, and crashed through her, taking him with her.

He pulled her hips down on his as he came in a spasm.

She jumped off him almost before he'd finished and collapsed at his side. "Bastard," she said between breaths.

"Bitch," he replied with an audible, annoying grin.

CHAPTER TEN

Three hours after she'd screwed him—a very hot screwing, at that—he'd woken from a light sleep to see the snow had stopped falling. He rose up on one elbow and saw Abby was still asleep. She looked like an innocent angel. He scoffed silently at that. *Yeah, right.*

He could just lie back down and go back to sleep. Clearly she wouldn't know any different. It wasn't his job to wake her so she could stop World War III—so *she* said. He lay back down, wrestling with his conscience. He wanted her out of his hair. No one made him admit he had a conscience, not without suffering the consequences.

He toyed with doing what he would usually. Fulfill the terms of his job and leave. He had indeed assured her safety—she'd proved amply that she could look after herself. But as she had said, he couldn't prove that unless she blew her cover with her father. Although he was pretty sure that covert operators were allowed to read-in their parents or spouses if they wanted to.

For a second he wondered if Baston already knew what his daughter did. But if that was the case, he wouldn't have wasted his resources making sure she was okay. *Bollocks.* He hated being against a rock and a hard dick. Hard *place.* Shit, his dick definitely was responding to her presence even if his mind was on her duplicity. Or maybe her little blackmailing soul was speaking to him. Maybe he liked being manipulated in such a blatant way.

He reached for her.

"You can stop right there." Her voice startled him. He dropped his arm to the covers.

"I was just going to shake you awake. You've been snoring like a bear," he said, swinging his legs out of bed.

She ignored his insult, such as it was. "You were supposed to wake me when it stopped snowing," she said, also climbing out of bed and seemingly not caring a whit that she was totally naked.

He sat still, taking in the sight. Her nipples puckering in the frigid air, her tight muscles moving in glorious efficiency. "It was your watch. Technically you should have woken me."

"Ass."

"Don't you forget it, love." He stood and got dressed, having dug out his Under Armour thermals from the kit bag he'd brought.

She poked her head around the bathroom door. "What? Don't forget what?"

"That I'm an ass. You've blackmailed me into helping you,

and someone as well trained as you knows that isn't a recipe for success." He finished tying his laces.

She shrugged. "I trust you."

"You shouldn't. I have a healthy regard for self-preservation and even I don't know what I'll do if you get in the way of that. So you're much better off not trusting me for anything. Just a friendly PSA." He knew he sounded like a dick, but he just couldn't help himself.

"I'm not worried. If you piss me off, or if you're in the way of *my* self-preservation"—she punctuated with air quotes—"or my mission, I won't hesitate to shoot you." She disappeared again.

"There's one problem with that, love. I've got your gun."

She didn't reply, but he heard the unmistakable sound of a shotgun being charged. "Fair enough," he said, trying not to smile at her resourcefulness. "What else have you got in there?"

"Hairspray," she said.

"Awesome." She was such a smart-arse. His sister would love her. He made a mental note that no matter what, they would never, ever meet. Ever.

She came out of the bathroom as if she'd come through a *Tomb Raider* portal. She wore a white snowsuit that matched his, a white knife strapped to her thigh, a white holster holding a white handgun under her shoulder, and a white shotgun on a white strap over her back.

"I'm sorry. The CIA gave you all that gear but couldn't give you a sat phone that worked? What the fuck?" Jesus. This was why he was in the private sector now. One too many times he'd been put in a sketchy situation without the right equipment. That didn't happen anymore.

She shrugged. "I guess they thought snow was more likely than the need to use an emergency phone?" She frowned, though, as if she was only just now considering that herself. "Are you ready to head out?"

He sighed, as if he was still being brought along against his will. "I suppose so." The future was a big blank book, and although he didn't mind traipsing along on her dubious "mission," he didn't like the arm-long list of unknown variables. He'd never before undertaken anything without knowing roughly what he was getting himself into. But this? Could be anything from random muggers coming back for revenge to getting cold, wet feet to World War III. Take your pick.

They used the stairs to exit her apartment building. The street was silent and dark. The power still hadn't come on, and the moon was so low it offered no light for the town. "Walk in the middle of the road as far as you can," he said, tugging on her suit.

"Why?" She pulled her arm away from him.

"Because there are more hazards on the pavement than there are in the road. Curbs, manholes, rubbish, dog shit." He grinned at her.

"You mean the sidewalk, I guess," she said tightly.

He sighed. "Really? You couldn't have made that intuitive leap in your own head?"

"I make it a habit to correct foreigners. It's the only way they learn." She walked a little faster. "I mean, don't you know the Queen's English?"

"Of course I do. She lives in Windsor. Haven't seen her passport, though, so I guess she could technically still be German, but I suspect we would have heard about it by now."

"What?" She sounded annoyed that he hadn't risen to her Queen's English comment.

"I know the Queen's English. She's the Queen of England—of course she's English."

"Oh, fuck off." She stomped ahead.

"I'm trying to. You just won't let me." He didn't know why getting a rise out of her made him so satisfied, but it really did. He barely even noticed the cold.

They made their way out of town. It was 3:00 a.m., and they hadn't yet seen anyone. Not even a flickering candle in the window. The air was frigid, and the only movement ahead of them was their breath crystallizing in the air.

She was almost paralyzed with the idea that she was going to get them both killed. Not that she minded a whole lot about getting Malone killed—he'd be lucky if she didn't do that herself—but if they died before finding out if Russia was actually invading Ukraine, she would have failed in her only mission. She wasn't prepared to do that, but her confidence in her decision to go marching across what might as well be the tundra in the middle of the night waned with every step they took into the frigid night.

Malone matched her footstep for footstep. She wondered if he'd have gone voluntarily with her if she hadn't essentially threatened his job. She'd never know now. And based on what little she knew about him, she could guess at the answer.

He said something she didn't hear. "What?" she said, not breaking stride.

"I wanted to go somewhere warm," he said.

She was about to dismiss his complaint as being whiny, when he continued.

"I already got frostbite in a cave in Afghanistan. I thought my freezing-my-nuts-off days were over. But then came you. Or rather, your father. And here I am. Makes me wish I hadn't met him. You know, I don't know much about the CIA, but I'm fairly sure that if you call them, you can get someone here to help you. It really doesn't need to be me. It never needs to be me. For the past six months I've been getting caught up in American messes. Why can't you guys ever do anything the easy way?" His voice had lowered, which made it sound as if he were a grumbly old mad muttering to himself.

She grinned. "For someone who claims not to know a whole lot, you certainly have a lot of opinions," she said. She wanted to roll her eyes at him, but she was worried in this temperature that they might stay rolled—giving credence to her second stepmother, who'd warned her that her eyes would stay that way.

He stayed silent, and suddenly she didn't want silence between them. It felt intimate, laden with unsaid things.

"I could have called someone for help. But no one would come on the basis of an alert on a pressure sensor that may or may not just be beeping to have its battery changed. I've changed some of them, but not all. If I call for help and it's nothing, I'll probably be reassigned to Greenland for the rest of my career. They didn't recruit me to scream for help at the first hurdle. They recruited me to handle shit like this." She watched her words leave her mouth as vapor, and then disappear. If only her words really ceased to exist after a few seconds. If only a lot of things did.

"You were recruited? You didn't apply?" he asked.

"Right out of high school. I did one semester of college while they went through the recruiting process and then went straight to the Farm." She'd been the youngest there by far, and that had isolated her. She couldn't go to the on-site bar, couldn't hang out with them outside class, and therefore had made few friends. A lot of them had been in government service for years in the military, police, or FBI. She'd been a kid. One they'd been suspicious of. One they'd condescend to at every opportunity. Suffice to say, she hadn't kept in contact with them when she'd graduated. The same uncertainty that she'd felt all through the Farm, she felt now. And she hated that.

"You must have been a real swot to be recruited from school," he said.

She bristled. "What do you mean, a swot?"

He hesitated. "A nerd? Someone who works all the time. It's English, love. You should try learning it." She heard his grin again, the one she was longing to smack from his face sometime soon.

"What about you? How did you end up in the SAS?" she asked baldly. If he wanted her to chat about her secret world, he'd better be willing to reciprocate.

"I was a squaddie right out of school. Just turned eighteen—"

"Squaddie?" she said. Her words were more difficult to push out with the exertion of wading through snow on an incline.

"An enlisted kid. The most expendable in the army. They send us in first in large numbers, and if you returned alive, you might get promoted." He didn't seem to be breathing as hard as she was, and that pissed her off.

"Go on." She tried to slow down a bit, to level off her exertion. She didn't want to be too tired when they got to the border.

He slowed down to keep pace with her. "I kept coming back. My ranking officer asked me if I'd considered joining the Regiment." He gave a short laugh. "That's kind of like asking a boy if he'd ever thought about being Superman. We all did. But none of us ever expected to actually do it. Back then, people regularly died just training for the opportunity to try out."

"And you were prepared to die just to find out if you were eligible to join?" She'd have been frowning if her face hadn't been immobile. You didn't need Botox in the winters here, that was for sure.

He didn't say anything for a minute, and when she looked at him he just shrugged. "I can't say I thought too much about it. When you're called to serve, you don't ask too many questions, do you."

Fair enough. "I didn't. I just accepted that if they wanted me, then I should join."

"So we're not too different." That grin again.

She stopped in her tracks, about to point out in no uncertain terms that they were so dissimilar that she couldn't even begin to list the ways, but he grabbed her and pulled her forward. "Don't stop. It's harder to stop and start. Keep going. You'll just have to be outraged on the move."

Damn him. He was even predicting her comebacks now. She tucked her head down and carried on walking. She wasn't going to dignify his comments with a reply. She wondered if she should try to use the satellite phone now that they were out of the city. But she still didn't have anything to tell them. When they figured out what was up with the sensor, she'd call. *When I figure it out,* she corrected herself.

"Can you feel that?" he asked.

A wind kicked up, first a breeze and then a rush of air so cold that her face—the only part of her that was open to the elements—throbbed with pain. And the wind meant snow. Another blizzard.

She turned to him and shouted into the wind, "We can't be too far from the orphanage. Let's speed up, try to get there before…" She didn't bother to finish her sentence, because large, wet blobs of snow were already blowing in their faces. "Shit."

"Just keep moving. Whatever happens, don't stop, okay?"

She nodded. In a few minutes even if they had spoken to each other, they wouldn't have heard a word. The wind blew the falling snow in their faces and the snow on the ground at their legs. What had she been thinking to embark on this stupid mission?

They walked for about an hour. At least that's what she thought. It could have been ten minutes; it could have been two hours. They had to be close to the orphanage. If they needed to, they'd hole up in the barn and wait for the blizzard to pass.

As she made that plan, the wind and snow stopped as if someone had flipped a switch.

"Watch out!" Malone's yell made her turn, but not before she felt the snow give way beneath one of her feet. He grabbed her and yanked her toward him, but his momentum forced him in the opposite direction and into the very crevasse he'd pulled her away from. As soon as she saw him fall, she knew it was the bank of a stream that ran alongside the road. At least it wasn't deep. She heard a splash, though. That wasn't good.

"Are you okay?" she asked.

He grunted as he pulled himself out. "Nothing a cocktail on a beach won't cure."

"Jesus, Garrett. Do you take anything seriously?" She stomped her feet to keep them warm.

"Not if I can help it," he said. "Come on."

Maybe he wasn't too wet. "The orphanage isn't too far. I wasn't going to go there, but maybe now..."

"I'm fine. Let's get this dog and pony show done so I can go back to civilization."

"Sure."

In the moonlight, she could see the outline of the orphanage and the barns and outbuildings that comprised the small farm. But she saw movement. "What's going on there?" She pointed.

Mal's only reply was a shrug.

She could see what looked like flashlights sweeping the

snow. Were the Russians already there? She ran forward as far as she could without being caught in the beams.

Voices called, "Dmitri! Lana! Dmitri! Lana!"

Her blood ran cold. The kids were missing? "Oh my God. The children are out in this?"

She made a split-second decision. She pulled off her snowsuit and handed it to him. "I'm going to distract them while you go to the barn on the right-hand side there. It's unlocked, and there's hay in there. Stay there until I come and get you."

"Roger that." He took her snowsuit without questioning her, which was strangely gratifying, and took her order like a...a squaddie.

She ran along the road, shouting for Tanoff's attention. "What's happened?" she called. The flashlights rested on her as she ran for the main house.

"What are you doing here? Dressed like that?" Tanoff demanded.

"I left my car on the road. I was coming tonight because I didn't think I would make it tomorrow. What's happened?" She rubbed her arms and tried to stop her teeth from chattering, avoiding his skeptical stare.

"We can't find Dmitri and Lana. They were so excited to see the snow, so I'm worried they could be out here. Go get a coat on and help us search. There's an electric lantern in the kitchen."

She couldn't imagine how the kids got out of the locked-up house even to play in the snow. But if they had, they needed to be found quickly. And, shit, she needed to be the one to check the barn. Her heart beat fast, and she tried to tamp down the fear she felt for the tiny children. Who could survive in this? She and Malone almost hadn't. She shivered at the thought.

She wrapped herself in one of Tanoff's coats and grabbed the portable light from the pantry. Running outside, she found Brigda searching the woodpile that extended from the house to the chicken coop. "Have you checked the barn?" she asked.

"Da. First look," she said, for once not pulling a face at the prospect of talking to Abby.

Thank God.

"Where do you want me to look?" she asked, wondering how far they'd gotten before she'd arrived. "Where do you want me?" she said louder, and faster, anxious to be given a task to help find them.

Tanoff came into view, and before Brigda could answer, he shouted, "Check the meadow."

She took one long look at the barn, hoping Malone would manage to stay warm, and ran down the pathway that she'd taken that very day to check the sensors. Her heart clenched at the idea that she might find them in the snow. There was no way they could dress themselves warmly enough to bear being out in this weather.

She halted in her tracks. There were no footprints anywhere between her and the meadow. She wondered if they'd gone missing before or after the blizzard. Or even if the blizzard had reached the farm.

She continued kicking herself for not asking before. She ran down to the field, which, although hidden by the topography from the main house, existed on a slope. She couldn't see any footprints, any—she gulped—child-shaped lumps in the snow. Just an even spreading of whiteness as far as the eye could see. She held up her lantern one last time and hoped that if there were in fact Russians gathering on the border, they wouldn't see her.

A shout came from behind her. It sounded triumphant. She ran back.

"All is good, all is good," Tanoff said, over and over. As she rounded the corner, she saw the two children in his arms as he rushed to the kitchen door. She ran to catch up.

"What happened? Are they all right?" she asked.

"Da. I think," Tanoff said. "In the chicken house. Making sure the chickens were warm."

Relief flooded through her. "Oh my God." She sank into one of the chairs around the kitchen table as Brigda opened the furnace door on her farmhouse oven. She stoked the ashes and added more wood. "Here. Help me," she said, holding blankets she'd taken out of the top oven. They were blissfully warm.

Abby grabbed the blankets and wrapped them around Lana while Tanoff did the same to Dmitri. She sat Lana on her knees in front of the open fire and rubbed the small of her back. A lot of blood rushed through veins that were close to the skin there. It was a good place to warm her up.

Tanoff watched her and did the same with Dmitri. Both children were awake but sleepy in a way that indicated the on-set of hypothermia.

"It seems they had gone to check on the chickens and then were too cold to come back. The chicken house was a little warmer than outside, though, so I hope no danger to them," he said, his English getting worse under the tension of losing the kids.

"They'll be fine now," she reassured him.

Brigda was making warm milk for them to drink and was heating up a big brass bed-warming pan in the open fire. "They sleep with us now," Brigda said to Tanoff in Ukrainian. "We keep them warm."

"Da," Tanoff said, holding a mug to Dmitri's lips. The little boy slurped the milk.

Brigda, now bereft of things to do, held her arms out for Lana. "You go now," she said to Abby in English.

"You can stay, Abby. Use the upstairs room." He nodded to her. He knew that she kept a computer and other equipment up there in the wardrobe, but presumably Brigda didn't.

"Thank you. I'm glad you found them."

As she left the kitchen, Tanoff stood with Dmitri still in his arms and told Brigda to bring Lana. They were going to bed too. Relief poured through her. The upstairs room meant that she could go and get Malone, and they could probably get upstairs without the couple knowing anything about it.

She waited until ten minutes had passed since their lights went off, then donned Tanoff's coat again and silently opened the kitchen door. She crept out into the night.

CHAPTER ELEVEN

Malone knew he was in trouble as soon as he got inside the barn. His wet legs had gone past pain and were completely numb. He took off his snow pants and rolled up his jeans. His legs were mottled and couldn't feel his touch. He rubbed them gently, trying to urge blood through them again. He'd also stopped shivering. He recognized all the signs.

Things were not looking good. But he'd had no alternative other than going on after he'd fallen into the stream. It wasn't as if he could have taken off his wet clothes.

There wasn't anything in the barn to keep him warm without setting fire to things, and that probably wouldn't be a good idea. He could hear voices calling but couldn't tell what they were saying.

He wondered what his sister was doing, but he couldn't quite figure out the time difference between Greece and the West Coast. But he wasn't in Greece now. He was in Ukraine with Baston's daughter. Abby. Lovely, bitchy Abby.

He wondered how much trouble he'd be in at work if he married her. Or if he died and left her to deal with the Russians herself.

He tried to dig his legs under some hay, but there wasn't enough of it. Then he pictured Abby, concern etched on her face, talking to him. Probably talking *at* him. Thank God his imagination had her on mute. He was sure she'd have little to say that was comforting. Not that he minded; he'd been trained to put the mission before his own comfort. They all had. The whole regiment.

Country first. Country first. Country…

He awoke to a pounding in his head and extremities. He felt like he was trapped under something heavy that was cutting off supply to his arms and legs and hands, and…

He half opened his eyes. Where was he? He lay perfectly still, eyes still closed, in case he'd been captured. Moments during which they thought you were still unconscious were valuable in ascertaining your surroundings. He breathed in slowly. Coconut scent invaded his nostrils as hair was inhaled into his mouth. He coughed and spat the hair out.

"Charming," the weight on top of him said groggily.

He opened his eyes. Abby's peered back at him from inches away. She blinked and yawned. "How do you feel?" she asked, rubbing her foot down one of his legs. Her hands touched his sides. "You don't feel as cold as you did when I found you."

"You found me? Wait, back up. What happened?" As he said the words, the night's activities became clearer. "Did you find the kids?"

She huffed out a laugh. "They were keeping the chickens warm, apparently."

"Good." His memory touched on the little boy who'd grinned at him when he'd been watching Abby in the fields. He wondered if it had been him.

He suddenly became aware that he was naked, and she was two small garments short of being naked. "Did you undress me?"

"Shhhh," she whispered. "They don't know you're here. I brought you in after they went to sleep. And, yes, I did undress you. You didn't tell me how wet you were last night."

He whispered right next to her ear. "To be fair, you never tell me when you're wet, either." The thought of her wetness, the two times he'd been close enough to touch her, made his dick stiffen.

She wriggled. "It feels like you're feeling better, soldier."

He stroked his fingertips down her sides, making her squirm against him. He was fighting a losing battle if he didn't want her to know how aroused he was. "So tell me what you did when you found me."

He felt her smile against his shoulder. She pulled away and rested her chin on the hand that was draped over his chest. "Well, when I came back to the barn for you, you were muttering, totally incoherently, about I don't know what. I managed to get you upstairs without anyone hearing, or at least coming out of their rooms to investigate."

She stroked his arm. "And then I sat you on this bed and undressed you. Rubbing parts of your body to try to get them warm. Like this." She took his hand in hers and she massaged it, rubbing the palm and the back of his hand until he was feeling the heat elsewhere. She blew on his fingers, holding them close to her mouth. Her tongue flicked out and licked the tip of his middle finger so quickly that he wondered if he'd imagined it. His body hadn't, though.

He knew she'd felt the twitch of his dick next to her leg when she repeated the lick. And then as he looked down at her lips, she sucked his whole finger into her mouth.

Heat flashed around his body in a way that he knew he'd escaped any serious cold-related injury. Hell, with Abby this close, how could he possibly be cold again?

He turned onto his side so they were facing each other. "You're a terrible person," he said in a very solemn, low voice.

She sighed. "Why, this time?"

He slid his hand beneath the covers and pulled her knee up, so it was propping up the covers, and then stroked down her thigh until he reached her panties. "Because your first thought when you woke up was to take advantage of a recovering man," he said, slipping his fingers beneath her panties. "You see? I told you that you never tell me when you're wet." He tut-tutted and shook his head as she arched into his hand, pushing for even more contact.

She slipped her leg over his hip and moaned softly when he stroked her clitoris through her wetness. He played lightly with it, reveling in its softness and her responsiveness.

"Do you want me?" he whispered.

She nodded, biting her lip in a way that made him need to lose himself in her. She took his dick in her hand and guided it against her.

With one motion, he was inside her. He put his mouth on hers to muffle a moan that shuddered out of her.

The bed was so small that all he could do was hold her against him as he thrust into her. Her tightness and heat wrapped around him made his world collapse into just him and Abby, fastened together, mouths together, swallowing each other's gasps. His fingers found her clit again, and as desperate as he was to taste her again, he wasn't leaving where he was right then. Buried deep inside of her, owning her, breathing her oxygen, and feeling her yield to his fingers…and his will.

She bit down on his neck as she rocked against him, dragging him closer to her with her leg still hooked over his hip. He was so close to coming, he thrust and held as his fingers slipped around her clit. Her gasps got louder, and as if she realized, she bit down again on his shoulder, and when she came, spasming around his dick, he rocked his pelvis against hers and came, deep, deep inside her, the pain of her teeth jagging heat along his spine with his climax.

He held her tight against him, not saying anything—not able to say anything that wouldn't ruin everything. He wanted her in his life. Well, in his house at least, and that was a big shift in his reality. And he intended to keep that to himself until death did them part.

Damn him and his fingers, and his dick, and his smart mouth. She snuggled next to him for a short moment, wondering for a second if this was what normal people felt. The warmth in a man's arms. A certain vulnerability that she'd never allowed herself to feel.

The irony that she was exploring these feelings with a man who was categorically the least likely candidate for comfort and security didn't escape her. Or maybe that was why she could explore her own vulnerability with him—because she knew it couldn't be real, that she couldn't rely on him. Although that was on her.

She rolled onto her back, with one leg out of the covers and off the side of the bed. There was nothing like blackmailing someone to help her with a mission and then wondering why she couldn't trust him. Yup, that was *all* on her. Why couldn't she have just been nice to him and politely asked for help? She was certain that's what normal people would have done. But normal had never really entered her world after high school.

She'd been petrified that she'd lost him when she'd gone to get him from the barn. He'd been alive but not coherent. It took the mother of all efforts to get him inside the house without making a noise. Her heart had hurt—she'd literally had chest pains, knowing that she'd put him back in the same position he'd suffered through in Afghanistan. Luckily he hadn't been able to speak as she'd taken off his clothes and tried to warm him with her body and the blankets.

Had she felt something for him? Or had it been a normal response to nearly losing a fellow human being? And a reluctant co-conspirator. One who made her laugh inside, even though she seemed to be perpetually rolling her eyes at him. He'd rescued her from falling in the stream. Put her well-being above his. What did that mean? Did he like her, even though she'd blackmailed him? It was all too much to take in.

Mentally shrugging, she jumped up and stretched. "Now if you could only produce a full breakfast and coffee from your snowsuit, you'd be the perfect way to wake up."

"Sorry, all my eggs broke when I fell into the stream trying to protect you. Eggshell everywhere, let me tell you."

She stopped. Maybe subconsciously she didn't want to owe him anything—but clearly she did. "That was very…" She dragged out the last word because she couldn't think of the right one. *Brave? Kind? Protective?* "…clumsy of you. But thank you nonetheless." *Why had she said that?*

He didn't seem at all bothered by her flippancy. He grinned. "Is there a shower around here?"

She pointed at a door. "The loft here is all set up for live-in help. But my boss didn't want me to live with them. I had information to dead-drop, and if I were living in, I wouldn't have the freedom of movement I do now. Well not *now*, now, obviously. Now we're stuck here until tonight. But we have a bird's-eye view of our target area."

Although the field adjacent to the house was hidden in a small dell, the border could be seen, marked by a row of hedges in the distance. She could see roughly twenty kilometers of border. The unmanned, largely unpopulated border. She sighed and turned back to him.

"You want to go first?" she asked.

"We could save water," he said with a cock of his eyebrow.

"Not really. Go see." She found a towel in a drawer and threw it at him. He strode naked from the bed to the tiny bathroom.

He poked his head back around the door. "I don't get it. Am

I supposed to kneel down or crouch? I mean, this is for humans, right?"

She rolled her eyes. "I'm sure you'll cope."

While he got clean, she took out her binoculars and computer. The PC wasn't linked to anything. When she'd mentioned Wi-Fi to the couple downstairs, they'd just looked blankly at her. But still, the binoculars recorded everything she saw, and after scanning the border, she hooked them up to the computer and downloaded what was there. Which was nothing so far.

When she eventually got back to her apartment, and if the snow gods were in her favor, she'd be able to upload it to the server. Then the analysts could…analyze it? She had no idea really, but she was sure that if she couldn't see anything, they wouldn't be able to either. Maybe it was just busywork designed to make them feel useful after months of being decidedly *un*useful.

Malone came out wearing a towel. He looked so damn masculine. Tanned, hair flecking his chest, and wet from the shower.

She swallowed and looked back out the turret window.

He slapped her ass. "Your turn. I left the water running in case they wondered what you were doing taking two showers."

"Thoughtful of you." She grabbed a towel from the same drawer and went to rinse off. When she reemerged, wearing the towel, he was already dressed. She'd hung his cold wet clothes on the antiquated radiator that was driven by the stove in the kitchen. She noticed that he'd put her clothes on there after he'd taken his.

"You look…clean," he said with a frown.

"Clean?" she said perplexed. Had he been about to say something else?

"I meant…warmer. You look warmer."

He was making zero sense. "What are you talking about? Did the cold get to your brain last night?" She turned to release her hair from the towel she'd wrapped it in to keep it dry.

He stood and wrapped his hand in her hair, suddenly standing so close that she had to take a step back. "Yes. It did. Or something did."

He leaned down and gently kissed her. At least his mouth was gentle, but his tongue was intent on its mission. Her knees suddenly felt as if she'd had too much vodka, and she had to lean on the edge of the small vanity next to the window.

He let go of her hair and took a step back. His attention seemed to have been grabbed by something outside, and he closed the curtains, taking most of the light from the room.

Deliberately he pulled the front of her towel and let it drop to the floor. The cooler air hit her skin with a rush of excitement. *She should complain, shouldn't she?*

But she didn't. Her gaze followed him as he touched the very tip of her nipple. "No, look at *me*," he said.

Her eyes met his as his finger swirled around first one nipple and then the other. He was still at arm's length. It was as if he was examining her. Like she was a project or a specimen. He took her arms and held them to her sides as he slowly dipped his head to take one of her nipples in his mouth. He sucked and then bit until she writhed against him. Then he simply stopped and lavished his attention on the other one.

Perched on the vanity, she felt more and more like an exhibit that he was experimenting on. She couldn't help herself, but she was so turned on by this…examination.

He nudged her legs open and pressed her back against the wooden top, which moved her pelvis forward. He hadn't said a word. He sat on the chair in front of the mirror and kissed her stomach. She clenched with desire. What was he going to do next?

He trailed a finger down from her navel to her open folds, his gaze fixed between her legs. "What are you doing?" she asked on a deep breath.

"Seeing you. The other times we've been together, you've insisted on turning your back or pretending to be angry, and now I want to see what you were hiding from me." He slid two fingers inside her and she instinctively opened her legs farther. With his other hand, he held her open. The touch of his hot tongue undid her. She all but whimpered under this…whatever this was. He licked her clitoris until she could barely stay perched on the furniture. And then he pulled away and stood.

He pulled her off the vanity and put his arm around her. He bent her back slightly and continued to watch her face as he manipulated her clit. She could feel her body lubricating his fingers as they glided over her.

"You're beautiful, love," he growled. "Your face is flushed, your eyes seem brighter. You seem more honest."

She tried to bring herself upright at his words, but he wouldn't let her. "No, you're not stopping me. It's not my fault that the truth hurts." He grinned, and with her on the brink of imploding, for once she didn't want to slap it off his face.

"Don't stop," she whispered.

The grin dropped from his face, and an urgency appeared. "I'm never going to stop, love."

As his fingers danced over her nerve endings, and his eyes never left hers, she felt as if liquid light were bubbling over inside her. She forced her gaze to remain on his as she came, falling into his eyes, his sudden sincerity.

She bowed forward, leaning her forehead on his shoulder as he gathered her in his arms. "See? That wasn't so bad, was it? A moment of honesty between us? You didn't even have to say anything."

She wanted to be outraged or to extract some kind of revenge, but she couldn't muster the energy. "Fuck off," was all she could murmur as she squeezed him.

"That's my girl." He squeezed her back.

Gah. No, she wasn't. But again, she couldn't say anything. Maybe she didn't want to say anything. Those moments looking into his eyes as she lay exposed to him had altered something. And until she figured out how to alter it back, she was prepared to take the path of least resistance.

God, he is so confusing. Or is it me who's confused?

She sighed and pulled herself away from him. There were noises from downstairs, and she figured it was time to make an appearance.

CHAPTER TWELVE

He had less than no fucking idea why he was suddenly determined to see behind the CIA operative's mask she kept so firmly in place. No idea why he seemed to be forcing her to participate in the one thing that he usually ran a fucking mile from. What was wrong with him?

He sat on the bed and buried his face in his hands. Okay, she may have accidentally saved his life. But he'd saved her from getting wet so…yeah, that didn't sound entirely equal. Then again, it was her fault he'd been hypothermic in the first place. Shit. Why should he be caring about this? Caring about where she fucking looks when he's getting her off?

Was it just because she was more interested in the mission than him? Which was a real turnaround on him. He'd lost count of the number of women he'd—what had she called it?—seduced and abandoned because of the mission he was on. Maybe he didn't want to allow her to do the same to him? Was that his ego talking? Or was it really because she wanted to admit that he meant something more than a means to an end?

Jesus, what was *wrong* with him?

He loved that she was combative with him; loved that she never backed down; loved that she knocked him on his ass in her apartment, pulled a gun on him, disabled those two guys single-handedly; loved her one-track mind—even when it was on the mission and not him; and loved that she relieved work pressure with sex, exactly how he'd always done.

What did that mean, though? Did he really care what it meant?

He hated that he'd left his bag in the barn; he had nothing to distract him up here. Abby hadn't come upstairs at all, so he hadn't been able to ask her to retrieve it either. So all he'd been doing is lying down, and every hour or so, he checked the border through the digi-binoculars. He had seen nothing, except a worrying band of heavy cloud, very slowly rolling toward them. Looks like they'd be enjoying another snowstorm as they searched for the Russian army. And nothing had ever gone wrong doing that.

He could kill Baston for not being able to see how capable his daughter was. Even if he didn't know she was with the CIA, surely he must be able to see that she could take care of herself? He had no earthly idea what he was going to put in his report to him when—if—he ever got to file another one. *Shit.* Baston was bound to call if he failed to turn in a report. And his phone was in the barn. Turned on. He looked at his watch and made the time zone connection. His report was a day late and a dollar short. Unless Baston had a hot date—which he usually seemed to—he would call to see where his report was, Mal was sure.

Suddenly, a beeping sounded from the corner of the room. Not a subtle beeping, but an aggravated beeping, like a smoke alarm. It was the same sound as the sensor had made in Abby's apartment. He jumped across the room and yanked open her bag, grabbing the sensor. He was fumbling to take the battery out when the door flung open.

It wasn't Abby.

He smiled. "Hi, how are ya?"

They were fucked.

The woman screamed.

Really fucked.

Tanoff was clearly stressed by the situation, and Abby didn't blame him in the least. He was pacing around the farmhouse table, putting his hand on his wife's shoulder whenever he passed her. For her part, Abby was trying to look as contrite as possible.

Malone was just sitting there with his chair pushed back far enough from the table that he could make a quick exit if necessary. Every bone in Abby's body wanted to do the same, but she knew the body language transmitted by sitting up against the table would give the couple a little comfort. Well, Tanoff at least. She wasn't sure if Brigda was going to be comfortable around her ever again.

"This is too much, Abby. You bring a strange man into our house. With the children around. What were you thinking?" He started pacing again. "You have to go."

"Please don't send us out into the blizzard. We walked here from town," she said.

"So you didn't come by car? Another lie?" he said, anger mounting in his voice.

Oh, you don't know the half of it.

"You know why I'm here," she replied in a calm voice.

The man's eyes darted to his wife's, but she didn't react to Abby's words.

"I don't care anymore. You can keep your money." He paced again, this time looking out of the kitchen windows as if he expected paratroopers to be hanging from helicopters above them. "If you bring trouble to our door…to the children…we won't be able to protect them."

"But if you let us say, we can help you protect them," she reasoned.

Malone stayed quiet, thankfully.

Tanoff's eyes were cold, and she felt like she was losing the argument. "At least let us stay until morning. Until the snow passes."

"Vot snow?" Brigda asked sharply.

"That snow," Malone said, pointing out the window. For a second nothing happened, but then a gust blew the first flakes against the pane.

She glanced at him. *How did you do that?*

He gave her an annoying smile. As more snow splattered against the glass, the children started to get restless in the playroom. Their excited chatter spilled down the hall to the kitchen.

Abby saw that as an opportunity. She stood up, startling

both Tanoff and Brigda. "I'll—*we'll*—look after the children for now." She nodded to Malone, who got up and was at the door before she'd even moved away from the table.

She followed him into the hall. Silently he took her hand and headed toward the playroom. Just before they got to the kids, Tanoff came out of the kitchen.

"Psht," he said, gesturing her back with a nod.

Malone looked at her, but she had no idea what Tanoff wanted. She shrugged and went back down the corridor.

"It's the first Thursday of the month," he said meaningfully before returning to his wife.

Oh shit.

She turned back to Malone, trying not to be scared.

"What did he say?" Malone asked before going into the playroom.

"Every month, their son—who's in the local police force —comes over for dinner with some of his colleagues." She pulled a face.

"Today?" he asked.

When she nodded, he sighed. "Awesome. Well, I'll just hide until they go. As long as you can keep your sensors from beeping."

It was a reasonable plan, but she was worried about Brigda. She worshiped her son and his police friends. Abby found it hard to believe that she wouldn't tell her son everything. Very hard. Maybe they just needed to leave. But go where? There was nothing between them and the border.

"You should go," she said, holding his arm. "This isn't your fight, and I'm sorry I got you into this. The last thing you need is to be sent to jail here in the winter. I mean, it's no picnic in the summer, but I can imagine—"

"Shush," he said. "I'm not going anywhere. If your sensors are working, this *is* my fight. Don't forget England is in Europe. I won't have Russia stomping over my continent. And if you're wrong, well, you'll owe me so big that you will spend the rest of your days constantly wondering how you can make it up to me." He pulled her close and whispered in her ear, "P.S., I already have plenty of ideas."

Relief flooded through her as she fought to keep tears from her eyes. "And if I'm right, you can spend the rest of your days wondering how you can reward me for saving your continent." She smiled and he squeezed her hand.

"Deal."

CHAPTER THIRTEEN

He was in no way delighted to watch her play with the children. And in no way did he enjoy playing with them himself. He wasn't amused by Dmitri's antics, nor was his heart squeezed when Lana, after two hours, eventually came over to show him her doll.

He didn't love drying their tiny hands before dinner, and he didn't like having to help some of them eat their fruit snacks. *Dammit. Yeah, right.*

He'd had no experience with children, other than once being one himself, and he'd never considered ever having anything to do with them. But seeing Abby being jumped on, having her long hair played with, and watching her stroke Lana's back so she would nap stole something from him. Maybe a degree of cynicism. Nothing more, though, he swore.

How had she managed to stay so mission-focused with these kids distracting her? And what did it say about his mission focus when all he wanted to do was watch her with the kids? This was where he should have had his cameras. Jesus. What was wrong with him? A question he'd been asking himself a lot since he'd met Abby.

She was strong and ballsy. Bitchy but kind. Hardheaded but considerate. A blackmailer. A hot, sexy blackmailer. And he was falling for her. There it was. He was nothing if not honest with himself.

They both went back up to the turret room while Tanoff and Brigda supervised the kids eating.

As soon as the door shut behind them, he took Abby in his arms and kissed her. Honestly kissed her. Not to distract her, not as a prelude to sex. He just wanted to kiss her. Because he wasn't sure he'd be able to protect her.

He pulled away from her.

"What was that for?" she asked, a gratifying flush tinging her face.

"It's probably going to go pear-shaped this evening. And I wanted to kiss you." He paused. "You know, in case we wind up in the gulag tomorrow."

"That is a strong possibility," Abby conceded. "I'm not sure Brigda won't be able to stop herself from turning us in to the police tonight. It's a bonus if her son can bring in the spies."

He sighed. "I know. But every mission I've ever been on had this possible ending. So we'll plan for the worst and hope for the best."

"We have a few hours," she said, looking at her watch. "Where do you want to start?"

"Well, I was going to say map of the border, but if we have a few hours, my plan has changed. Completely." He raised his eyebrows in a mock leer.

"Oh yeah," she replied with a grin. "A whole new plan?"

He laughed. "Nap time."

She pouted.

"If we are going to be up all night stopping a Russian invasion, or, you know, being interrogated all night by quasi-Russian police, I think we may need to be well rested." He pulled back the covers of the tiny bed, and they undressed silently. She left on her panties and bra, and they lay down, just as they had found themselves that morning. He set his watch and put it on the floor beside them. "Two hours, then one hour of planning, then it will be dinner with the enemy," he said. "For you anyway."

"Or am I sleeping with the enemy?" she countered drowsily.

"*An* enemy, perhaps, but not *the* enemy. So, you know, it's okay."

"'kay."

He wrapped his arms around her and pulled her on top of him, her legs tangled in his. Her heart beat against his sternum, and the steady thump lulled him to sleep.

He silenced his phone as soon as it beeped, but Abby had been awake thinking about their evening activities. She was going to skip dinner. It wouldn't be weird because she'd only ever been there for dinner one time since she'd been there.

If they both were able to keep quiet, maybe they could slip out while the family was eating. Then there'd be nothing to worry about. Except being caught. Being ratted out by Brigda, or being captured by the Russians.

"Are you awake?" he asked, his voice rumbling through his chest where her head was currently resting.

"Mmm-hmm," she replied, enjoying her low level of consciousness too much to want to speak just yet.

His arms squeezed around her once, and then he stroked her back. It felt loving. As if she were cared for. She would take all she could get, because she could be dead tomorrow.

Although wasn't that always true? Even if she had the most boring office job in the agency, she could as easily be run over by a bus as be killed on a mission. Maybe she needed to seize life a little more. Be cared for. Care for someone. Maybe that didn't necessarily mean that she'd lose focus. Maybe she could focus on more than one thing? Did she want to, though?

She roused and propped her head up on her elbow. "I think I should go downstairs and make my excuses. If I don't turn up for dinner, no one would be surprised, because I'm rarely here, and we can sneak out while they're eating."

"Sure, if you think they'll let you get out of it. We can be quiet up here. Look, it's getting dark now. Maybe we can even get out before they arrive," he said, sitting up in bed.

"Let me slip on some clothes and go down and tell them I won't be there. I'm sure they'll be happy to get rid of us. I'll be right back to make a plan with you." She smiled. "A real plan."

"Roger that, team leader." He yawned and stretched, and suddenly she wanted to do nothing but stay in bed with him and kiss his chest and talk about things. Things like his favorite football team. Or maybe soccer team. About his family. Favorite vacation places—although she had a feeling he'd taken far fewer vacations than she had, and she'd taken two in the past ten years.

She fought the urge to kiss him and got up, slipping her socks and jeans on and pulling a turtleneck sweater over her head. "I'll be back in a few."

He saluted her as she left the room.

She wasn't back in a few.

She ran downstairs, through the hallway and into the kitchen, slipping on the tile floor as she tried to stop.

Uh-oh. Her heart started racing.

Four police officers sat around the table with shot glasses of vodka in front of them. They all shuffled to their feet when she entered the room. There was no getting away from this one. Shit, and they hadn't even made a plan. One of the men still had his shot glass in his hand, and he raised it to her. She smiled in response and sat at the table, making them all sit too.

So far, so good. They hadn't rushed her and handcuffed her, so Brigda must have held her tongue so far. Tanoff put a shot glass in front of her and filled it, then went around the officers, filling theirs too. She raised her glass to the couple's son and downed the liquor in one gulp.

The men laughed loudly and did the same. The older man refilled the glasses again from the bottle Tanoff had left on the table. "Is too cold not to," he said in fragmented English.

"Da!" She grinned, taking a slightly more reasonable sip this time. She didn't want to be dancing-on-the-tables tipsy tonight of all nights. Although if Brigda did decide to break the news over dinner, at least she'd have a cushion of alcohol for any interrogation.

She caught Tanoff's eye. He raised another shot glass in question, and she shook her head, just enough for him to see. Maybe if she could get the policemen drunk, that would serve her well too.

Brigda refused to meet her gaze, which still gave Abby concern. The conversation revolved around the snowstorm and the electricity still being out in town. One of the policemen thought that maybe the Russians had shut off power because the Ukrainians had done the same to the Russian-occupied Crimea. The others laughed at him, saying that their town wasn't big enough for any country to worry about. They couldn't even get the Ukrainian government to pay for new roads. If the Russians wanted to retaliate, they would try to hack the power grid in Kiev, of course.

Abby smiled as she listened, not reacting to anything they said. What they weren't thinking about was that a town right next to the border, without power to communicate, would be important to the Russians. She hadn't even thought about it before, but it made perfect sense. More sense than the snow blowing out the electricity. This area of Ukraine had snow sometimes eight months of the year. She caught Tanoff's eye and stared meaningfully at him. He also knew why they would be interested in this small town. She just hoped he was on her side when push came to shove.

She itched to go back to the room and tell Malone. If they had shut off the grid, there was zero doubt in her mind they were about to do something bad—like invade. All the Russian president wanted was to make the USSR whole again. And all NATO wanted was to stop that from happening.

Brigda dished out food—the best food was always saved for her son and his…Abby wanted to call them comrades, but she wasn't sure if they were pro-Russia or pro-separatist. They gave no hint. Excitement and fear battled for supremacy as she forced herself to eat and smile and drink. Everyone seemed to be relaxed and having a good time, except Brigda and Tanoff; she hoped their son would think the tension lay between them, rather than having anything to do with her.

She kept an innocent smile on her face and widened her eyes to give an open expression, but every time Brigda said something or even opened her mouth to eat, Abby's stomach twisted. She hoped Malone would realize what had happened and was making a plan, because with as many eyes as were on her right now, she could only think about running for the door and shouting "run" to Malone too. Some plan that would be.

As Brigda brought dessert to the table, and more vodka for the glasses, Abby started to relax. There would be no reason for her to suddenly blurt out that spies were in the house now, would there? Not when they were so close to leaving. Relief made her giggle.

Everyone stopped and stared at her. She should have been mortified at the attention, but she giggled again. Then she looked aghast at the five empty bottles of vodka on the windowsill. There were seven of them at the table. Which meant there was a chance that she'd drunk half a bottle of ninety-proof liquor. Hell.

She giggled again and pressed her hand to her mouth. Suddenly the men started laughing too. Brigda and Tanoff were unmoved and looked disapprovingly at her. Shit. That would tell their son quite clearly that she was the problem in the house.

She stood up. "Excuse me…I should go and leave you to…drink." This time she manufactured a giggle and raised her glass to them. They all bid her good night loudly, and she escaped.

She closed the door quietly and waited for a second. The conversation resumed behind her as she tiptoed down the corridor to the stairs. She was halfway up the first flight when someone said her name. It was the son. She searched for his name. Anton. That was right.

"Is everything all right, Anton?" She smiled.

He ran his finger beneath his collar as if he were hot or uncomfortable. "Do you know what has happened with *mama a otets*?" He'd slipped into plain old Russian, not the Ukrainian hybrid language his parents used. She hoped that wasn't a bad sign.

She thought fast. "Your parents had a bad night. Two of the children sneaked out into the snow. We couldn't find them for ages and I think it affected your parents." She paused. "They were in the chicken coop, keeping the chickens warm." She smiled. "You should leave soon before the snow makes the road impassable. Good night." She turned and took two steps.

"Don't worry about us. We are staying the night. That is why all the vodka." He cocked his head. "Must you go?"

Nothing was going to go right for them. This whole mission was jinxed. Doomed. She forced a pout. "I must, yes. The children get up early. I'll try not to let them wake you."

This time she took the stairs with purpose to stop him following her. She paused before taking the turret steps until she heard his footsteps disappear back down the corridor.

She took a breath. Once upon a time, and it felt like years ago, she'd wondered if it could have been worth striking up a relationship with him, given his rank with the local police. Now she was glad she hadn't. That would have been a complication too far.

She knocked gently and then opened the door to the small room.

"Jesus. I thought I'd lost you," Malone said, wrapping her in a hug. "I was giving you ten more minutes before coming for you."

"They were all already there. Anton plus three other police officers. The worst thing is that they are all staying the night." She pulled away to see his expression, to see if he was as scared as she was.

"That's not the worst thing. The worst thing is you stink of alcohol. How can you drink when you know we're spending the night in freezing temperatures? Alcohol can lower your body temperature even further in the snow. You should know that." He held the tops of her arms and shook her to get her attention.

"I know that. I couldn't not drink. They were toasting and pouring. It was already tense down there; I didn't want to stick out in any way. Listen. We have to go. Brigda didn't say anything over dinner, but who knows what might be discussed when they continue to drink after dinner? Besides, there's no way we'll get out if we wait for them to go to bed. Someone is bound to hear us."

"Okay, let's suit up."

She was gratified that he wasn't going to argue the point with her, despite the fact that she still felt a little woozy from the vodka. He was right—that had been a boneheaded move. But there was no use crying about it now. They had to get out there to the border. "What's the plan, Stan?"

CHAPTER FOURTEEN

If you need evidence that the Russians are on the border, and it is really them—although everyone knows it is—then we've got to go and get photos of something that says Russian troops," Mal said.

"Then we have to get it uploaded in a farmhouse with no Internet, and a town with no power. How hard can that be?"

He grinned as she mocked him. None of this was going to be easy.

They slipped back into their snow gear and he watched admiringly as Abby strapped on her guns. He still had some of his things stashed in the barn, so the plan was to grab those on the way out. He'd had one opportunity to go get them but didn't want to risk bringing more guns into a house with a lot of small children.

Once kitted up, they made their way downstairs, using the front door, which Abby had said was rarely used and farthest away from the kitchen. By the sounds of it, people were still there drinking. Getting out was easy. The wind was blowing and absorbing any noise they made. Getting around to the barn was a different matter. The kitchen windows looked out to the barn. They just couldn't risk it, so they made tracks away from the house and down into the meadow, which was hidden from the whole house except the turret.

For a nice change in luck, the wind was at their backs, making it easier to see and easier to progress. Maybe this was where their luck changed. Maybe they could get this done, get back to civilization, and spend time together before either of them got shipped out to their next job. That was if he still had a next job when Baston read his reports, which now that he thought about it, would have to sound as if he'd dragged Abby into the World War III business and not vice versa.

He shrugged. He was just a tad beyond caring what Baston believed was going on here. He was so fired.

"Are you okay?" Abby shouted into the wind as she looked back.

He gave a thumbs-up and caught up with her. By his estimation, they still had about two hours of walking to go, more if the wind changed.

But it didn't. Their luck held. For once.

There was a wooded area to their right, and he grabbed Abby's arm and pointed her toward it. They needed cover to see what they needed to photograph. No sense in wandering up and down the border crossing and hoping no one would see them.

They crouched in the small glade of trees, digging out snow and trying to find some non-icy floor for their hideout, because God alone knew how long they'd be there.

After watching Abby wriggling into a half-dug hole between a bush and a low-hanging tree, he crawled in after her. There was room enough to crouch and sit out the snowfall. As soon as the blizzard stopped—and he hoped it did soon—they could scope out the border line. They were maybe thirty meters from it, but visibility was still virtually nil.

Abby took her hood down and put a headband on that covered her ears. She looked as if she were about to go skiing.

"I wish we had the luxury of a weather forecast. I just want to know if we'll be sitting here for hours or days."

"Could be either," he said.

"How very intuitive of you." She grinned and tugged her shotgun from her back and put it in front of her.

There was silence between them for a minute as they looked out toward Russia.

"Where's home for you?" he asked her.

She frowned. "The apartment in town. Hint: You've. Been. There." She started rummaging in her tiny backpack for something.

"No, I mean when you're in the U.S.," he said.

She shrugged. "I don't know. I don't have anywhere. What about you?"

"I have a flat in London and an apartment in D.C., where your father's office is. Although, when he gets to hear about this, I doubt I'll be needing the apartment in D.C."

"Awww, don't be like that," she said. "I'll make sure you still have a job."

"How? You'll tell your father that you're a highly trained CIA operative?"

"No, of course not. I've told you that already. I can't tell him without losing my own job."

He cared less about that than her not having a home. "You seriously don't have stuff in the US? No apartment? What about a storage locker?"

She settled back into the makeshift foxhole and turned to face him.

"I get that you think because I'm posing as an aid worker that I must have a different life somewhere—but I don't. Even though I'm playing a part, most of the time, this is still my life. If I put some imaginary life on hold in the US while I'm working, then I'll never feel like I'm living the life I have here—or wherever they send me next. I have to live my life where I am, or I'll never really be living. Does that make sense?"

In a very sad way, maybe. Or perhaps it wasn't sad at all. Perhaps this life in her apartment was a fulfilling one. He just didn't know. "It does make sense, actually. So what do you do to make your fake life real? Do you have hobbies, things you like doing while you're undercover?"

She hesitated. "Not…really. I actually don't have much time to do anything else here. While I was in Moscow, I learned how to tango and play a mean game of darts, but here there's not been much time for any of that."

"Darts, huh?" he said, even though his mind was on her

in a long red dress dancing a tango, rose between her teeth. *Rose between her teeth?* "Can you play Killer?" he asked, referring to a specific type of pub darts, and needing to change the subject.

"I don't *play* Killer." She shook her head in pity. "I *own* Killer," she said with triumph in her eyes.

"Challenge accepted. Next time you're in London, we'll see if you live up to the hype. Be careful what you bet me."

"You be careful what *you* bet. Be sure you're ready to lose it too."

A short silence fell as he put the digi-binoculars up to his eyes and scanned the horizon. The snow was getting a little lighter. "Bloody hell," he whispered slowly before shoving the glasses at Abby. There were armored vehicles stretched as far as the eyes could see. Which, to be fair, wasn't that far in the snow.

"Shit," she whispered back. "I wanted to be wrong. I really wanted to be wrong."

"Do you see any personnel?" he asked.

"None in sight."

"You need to call this in," he said, stating the obvious.

"Really? I thought I might go take one for a joyride," she murmured. She pulled out her antiquated cell phone and dialed. He could hear the static from where he was sitting.

"Give it ten minutes. It looks as if the sky is clearing." He nodded toward the rear of them, where the moon was shining behind dashing clouds.

He watched as she fidgeted, eyes to the sky, waiting for the clouds to pass. The snow had already stopped, but she still managed to look like an angel on a Christmas card, with bright eyes and snowflakes on her eyelashes. He wanted to brush them off, but it felt uncomfortably like what someone in a romantic comedy would do. Not that he'd ever watched any. Nope. Maybe one or two—when there was nothing else on. He deliberately looked away. He was trying hard not to get involved with her op—whatever that turned out to be.

It did look like she was right on the money, though. White armored trucks, hiding in the snow. He thought about the implications. Now that he was here, looking at the huge vehicles, none of it seemed entirely clear. He wasn't sure about the capabilities of those vehicles, but he wasn't sure that one could actually invade another country successfully with them. It's not like they were tanks.

"I've got a signal," she said. He wondered what her boss would ask her to do, and by implication what he'd have to do. There was no way he had time to render all the vehicles undrivable. And the two of them against the number of troops it would take to drive and man them sounded like a suicide mission.

"Kate? Kate, thank God," she said.

He raised his eyes to the sky and prayed that she wouldn't be ordered to do anything suicidal, because he knew right now that he wouldn't let her go alone. Wouldn't let her fight this battle alone. Wouldn't let her get shot. And shit. Would he take a bullet for her? Would he let his finely honed survival instinct take a backseat to protect her? Was he in love with her? He kicked the ground in front of him, making

Abby glance quickly at him. He smiled. "Spider," he whispered.

She pulled a face and continued talking to Kate.

Fuck. Fuck. He *was* in love with her. He waited for the fear to permeate his already-frozen body. The fear of commitment, of the thought of caring enough about another human being that you'd rather take a bullet than see them take one.

It didn't come.

"Dammit, Kate. You're breaking up. Speak slower." It seemed that Kate had been holding in a two-day panic that was now being released in a rush down the phone.

"I'm sorry, sweetie. I just thought something may have happened." She seemed to swallow. "I knew there was a snowstorm…I knew it. I just don't like knowing I can't get hold of you."

"I would have emailed, but the town lost power too. In fact, you should look at that. There is thought around here that the Russians hacked the town's grid to prevent any communication. I'm at the border right now and there are very large armored trucks and other vehicles lined up as if they're about to cross into Ukraine. What do you want me to do?" Abby took a breath. There was no sense muddying Kate's mind with the fact that there were police and an annoyed woman at the orphanage. One who might snitch on her at any moment. Or the fact that she had some non-official company. She cut her eyes to Malone, who was staring at the sky. She looked up, too, just in case she was missing paratroopers dropping from an aircraft. Nope. Now he seemed to be look-ing at the border.

"I'm going to give you directions in sixty minutes—"

Static buzzed for a couple of seconds and then there was silence. She looked at the brick of a phone. It was dead. "Son of a…," she said. "The battery's dead. I charged it last night. I don't understand." She shook it, frustration crush-ing her. They would have to walk back to the farmhouse in order to charge it, but they'd never make it back in an hour. "Fuck."

"She said she would be giving me orders in an hour." She knew she didn't have to explain anything else to him—he'd pick up all the implications.

"Everything loses its charge faster in low temperatures. Even me," he said with a cocked eyebrow.

"I find that hard to believe. At least of you." She shoved the dead phone back in her pocket. "Hmmmm," she said, follow-ing Malone's line of sight.

He nodded, still watching the line of vehicles. "Maybe we can borrow one?"

Abby squinted at the armored vehicles. "I've seen no troops here. It's like a parking lot."

"And why armored vehicles?" he asked quietly.

Shit. He was right. Why armored vehicles instead of tanks? The Russians had over fifteen thousand tanks, and they had been impossible to stop when they invaded Crimea, the south-ern part of the Ukraine. So why the hell were they using ar-mored vehicles here if they were planning to invade? Why wouldn't they have their tanks lined up? "Ohhhh."

Malone got up. "Right. Let's test this theory. Let's see if anyone's here."

Before she could stop him, he'd jumped out of the foxhole and into the moonlight. She winced, staying put for a second, and then realized that she wasn't going to sit there while he put himself on the line for her mission. She climbed out, holding her gun at eye level, scanning the vehicles and her heart slowing with the anticipation of gunfire. None came. Not even a sound. No exhaust was being emitted, so none of the vehicles were on. There were also no footprints.

She lowered her gun. As she did, Malone turned around and looked at her. He shrugged and tucked his gun in his snowsuit pocket. "There's no one here. Literally no one." She caught up with him as he was scraping the snow from the side windows with his arm and looking inside.

"Empty."

He strode along the length of the line, counting as he went. "Fifty-six," he shouted back at her. She tucked her own weapon away and one by one, started scraping the snow from the driver side window, looking for keys left inside.

She found them in the eleventh vehicle. The door opened as if it was on hydraulics. Nice, better than the ones she'd been in before. They needed an act of God to open or close the doors. Jesus, the Russians had upgraded their military. Not just tanks that couldn't be stopped, but also nifty armored cars too. She got in and turned the key. It started beautifully the first time.

She got out and beckoned to Malone. "Come on, let's go!"

"Tell me you hot-wired it. That would be such a turn-on,"

he said as he jogged to the passenger side of the truck.

And it was such a turn-on for her that he didn't automatically try to drive.

They got in and closed their doors with a swoosh. He raised his eyebrows at her and she nodded. "I know. Nicer than anything I've sat in on the job."

"Worryingly enough, me too. Our armored stuff works great, but nothing about them is easy or comfortable." He pressed a button to lower the window to rid it of the snow. "When did they upgrade? I mean, last I paid attention to them, they couldn't afford to pay their troops. And now they have state-of-the-art equipment. I'm suddenly concerned."

"Me too," she said, slipping it into gear and crossing the border. As she did, she wondered…was she now a Russian agent by bringing one of its vehicles across the border? If the Ukrainians were all over this, would they open fire? She glanced at Malone, who seemed more interested in checking out the controls and the capabilities of it than the geopolitics of their borrowing it.

The progress was slow, as she didn't want to risk running into a ditch or anywhere that would hamper their journey back to the farmhouse. If they didn't get to the phone, NATO could be mobilized to the border. Which twenty minutes ago, she wanted. But now she realized this whole operation with the armored vehicles had been one hell of a decoy.

"Just a distraction," she muttered, shaking her head.

"What? What did you say?" Suddenly all of Malone's attention was on her.

"This whole thing was a distraction. They put their armored vehicles here so they can really invade somewhere else. *Fuck.*" She didn't know if she was upset that she couldn't stop an invasion or upset that all the time she'd spent here was a wasted op. Well, maybe not wasted if she could warn people about it.

"My last job, I was in Athens for the G20 meetings," Mal said. "I kind of got involved in a thing there. Some Russians were going to blow up the Russian embassy."

"Wait. The *Russians* were going to blow up the *Russian* embassy?"

"Yup. When we caught the people involved, all they would say was, 'It was just a distraction,' and at the time, we couldn't figure out what it would have distracted us from, because nothing else happened during the G20 meetings. Maybe they were setting a series of distractions to keep everyone looking in one direction—or multiple directions—and not looking at where the action really was."

"We have got to get word back. Otherwise we will have played right into their hands. *Dammit.*" She slammed her hand on the steering wheel.

Malone reached over and took her hand, rubbing his gloved thumb over her palm. Warmth slowly pushed through her, along with a reassurance.

"Thank you for doing all this with me," she said in a low voice.

He laughed, almost too heartily. "What are you talking about? You didn't give me a choice, remember? You were going to get me fired if I didn't help you!" He took his hand back and looked out the window.

It was as if she'd accidentally switched him off. The nice Malone, that was. What had she said? She'd thought that maybe they'd found some weird connection, so unlikely in their field. But as with freaking everything else in the past week, she'd been wrong. "Too right. I was just being nice. After all this traipsing around in the snow, nearly getting you killed, I thought it polite to thank you."

"Well, thank you. That's the first time I think you've shown your polite side. It's noted."

Abby stiffened. Why was he suddenly being such an ass?

CHAPTER FIFTEEN

Jesus. Why was he being such a wanker? It was like a compulsion. He'd been fine being kind to her before he acknowledged that he might have feelings, and now he had no control over how fast his mouth was backpedaling.

"You know, you didn't have to keep fucking me if you were only here under protest. Unless you were suffering from Stockholm syndrome?" Her voice was as frigid as the night air.

He wanted to placate her, to soothe the spikiness of the mood in the vehicle as it bumped over God knew what, plowing through the snow. "Look. I did what you asked me to. The mission's nearly over. Let's not allow tantrums to get in the way of the endgame."

"Tantrums?" she nearly yelled. "What the fuck are you talking about? Are you talking about me having a tantrum? Is there any way for you to be more condescending?"

"Okay, maybe that was the wrong word. Let's just get this

finished. One call to your masters and we should be all free to go back to the way things were before."

"Before?"

"I don't know, but I seem to have divided my life between preblackmail and postblackmail. So when you make your call to whoever pulls your strings at Langley, I will go back to my apartment, write my final report, telling your father that you are able to take care of yourself, and call it a day. Maybe get to go back to Greece, where the beaches, and women, are always warm." What the fuck was he saying? He had to stop. Just stop speaking.

"I'll be able to tell my father a fair few things about you, too, don't forget. How you screwed me every chance you got and then just left when the job was done. My *father's* job." She spoke between gritted teeth.

"So that's it, is it? We're back to the blackmail? What's wrong with you? I've been risking my life for you for the past few days, risking my limbs, which I doubt would take to frostbite a second time without needing to chop the fucking things off…I've had your back, and all you've got for me is 'I'm going to tell Daddy'? It's pathetic." Okay, now heat pulsed through him and not in a good way. His temper was getting dangerously close to the surface, and if he wasn't careful, he'd start punching things again. He wondered if the swanky new armored vehicle would stand up to the assault he badly wanted to unleash on it. *What is wrong with me?*

His carefully tucked-away fury unfurled in his chest, spreading heat through him. This wasn't like him. No one who knew him could ever say he was one to lose his temper. Not that he let people close. His anger never surfaced. Never. But it kept bubbling up, like an untamed geyser.

"It seems to be the only reason you're here, isn't it?" she shot back. "You call yourself a soldier? You'd be ready to go back to the bar, pick up some woman, drink some cheap booze, and just wait for war to break out. Why would you care? You gave up service. At least I still know about loyalty, patriotism…" She bit out every word, and he couldn't help wondering whether she'd been thinking about this all along.

"Don't you dare talk to me about patriotism. You have no idea what you're talking about, and no fucking clue about me. Just because you shagged me doesn't mean you're an expert on me now. For your information, in the UK we're taught to think for ourselves, not just blindly repeat pledges and doctrines. You're a fucking sheep is what you are. A scared sheep at that. Remember who was fucking whimpering when she thought I'd left her? That was you, love. You're just a scared little girl." *For the love of God, shut up. Shut up now.*

"You think this scared little girl would want to go to a beach when Russia is about to invade a European country? I thought you cared about that shit. You told me you did. Or was everything out of your mouth a lie? What am I saying? Of course it's a lie. It's what you do."

"It's what I do? What does that even mean? I work for your father, that's it."

"And you've never lied to me?" she scoffed.

"I've never—" He hesitated. Did a lie of omission count?

"Exactly." She sounded triumphant, and that burned him. She really thought everything out of his mouth was a lie?

"I've been utterly truthful to you about everything, except one thing I didn't tell you—because you didn't need to know. And you still don't." No! He'd opened the door. He never wanted to tell her that she'd killed one of her muggers. She didn't need to know. Still didn't.

She swallowed. "I knew it. My father has a habit of taking on fuckups and trying to make them worthy. Guess it didn't work for you, did it? Is that why you got this gig? You're ex-SAS and you're sent to watch me from across the street. I guess he didn't trust you with anything...I don't know...important?"

"All right. Stop the fucking car. I'm going to walk back to my apartment and pretend I never met you. I think that would probably serve you better right now. You can't want a fuckup around your mission. I'm out of here."

She slowed to a stop. "Oh, sure, sure. Run and hide."

Belying the emotions roiling in him, he calmly got out. "You should watch your right hook, love. You killed one of your muggers. Nasty business." He slammed the door and started walking. As she drove by, he just kept his head tucked down. Baston didn't pay him enough to take this shit.

Except he did. Every day. Dealing with shit was his specialty. How had he let her get under his skin like that? So she insulted him, called him out on his work record, his patriotism. Claimed he'd only been hired because he was a screwup. Well, everyone in his line of work was. Everyone. That's how they could do the things they could do.

He stopped and looked up. Fuck. She'd probably struck out because she was scared. And he had done nothing to soothe her. He'd just riled her up even more, and why? Because he was fucking scared of the feelings that he had for her.

Nuts. It was all wrong; they weren't supposed to be together. The very thought was crazy. They led different lives—his centered on holding down his job and trying to do a bit of good in the world, and hers was centered on where the CIA would send her next. Judging by what she'd said, she didn't seem to rate him too highly. Just as a hired gun for her father. And she was probably right. But all that aside, he'd just let her take on the Russians by herself because she hurt his feelings. And that was a wuss move.

What just happened? She drove on autopilot toward the orphanage so she could charge her phone without getting stuck in the snow on the way back into town. She'd killed someone? He just dropped it on her and left? Her hands shook no matter how tight she held the steering wheel.

She'd known that there was a possibility that she'd have to kill someone in her line of work, but she'd always assumed that it would be a terrorist or to stop something awful from happening. She didn't imagine she'd do it with her bare hands, just to prevent being a victim of a common mugging. Why had he told her?

Because you were acting like a spoiled child. You know better than to accuse anyone of being a fuckup, let alone a black-ops combat veteran who had seen who knew what in his career. Done who knew what. She was truly the worst person in the world.

The burn in her stomach was still there. She'd wanted to hurt him for hurting her. And she had. And he'd hurt her right back again. That was a cycle that would never stop.

She'd only known him for a few days and she already felt his presence under her skin, like a warm protective layer…and she hadn't realized it until he'd left.

Until she'd made him leave, if she was being honest with herself.

She'd grab his phone from the barn, make her call, and then go get him. Apologize. Grovel. Whatever it took to have him hold her again.

She cruised to a halt on the far side of the barn. Darkness still invaded the farm, with icicles twinkling in the sporadic moonlight. It looked like a perfect Christmas scene. Quiet and calm. She hoped everybody was sleeping off the effects of the vodka.

If she were lucky, she'd be home and making up with Mal within an hour. She grinned and stretched. That sounded like the perfect end to a perfectly weird day.

She stepped quietly around the piles of snow to the front of the barn. She pulled the door open at the exact same time as she saw a mass of footprints leading inside. Fuck. She'd been careless—her mind on Malone. It was too late. Three sets of guns trained on her.

Anton and his three friends, except Anton hadn't even bothered to draw his gun. He held his arms out like she was his long-lost…lover? She cringed. What had she done? Jeopardized the mission, sent Mal away, and now she couldn't call to warn Langley about the Russians' attempt at distraction. Had her base lack of protocol caused war? The very thing she was sent to avoid?

"We were so worried about you when I came to your room and found you gone," he said.

"Why did you come to my room?" she hedged. She could get out of this, she was sure.

He cocked his head. "Why do you think?" he asked almost coquettishly.

Oh Lord. She dipped her head as if she were embarrassed. "I don't know."

But this wasn't a flirtation, even if his coming to her room had started out as one. She could see that now. The other men trained their guns on her, with eyes that said they were a hop, skip, and a jump away from lighting her up. She reached her hands up. "Hey—I'm not dangerous, I promise," she said with a conversational tone and an expression that invited them into the humor of the situation. *Four men against little ol' me.*

There was silence, and she started to see a slightly bigger picture. She'd just arrived in a Russian army armored truck. Under normal circumstances, that would be very bad, or very good, depending on where their sympathies lay. Maybe she could play on that. If they were Russian sympathizers, they might be friendly to someone who appeared to also be one. But then if it went the other way, she could be sent to a Ukrainian city jail, and that was about as good as it sounded.

She needed to figure them out. Get them talking.

She slowly brought her hands down with a smile. Two of the men ignored her move, but the third came to attention, leveling her in his gun sight. She flared her hands at her side. "Remember? Not dangerous." She smiled again. And then remembered how much they'd all been drinking mere hours before.

Anton nodded to one of the men, who brushed past her to release a hatch in the barn floor. Under the hatch was some kind of dark…oh no. She wasn't going down that hole without a fight. Her heart clenched. And then her stomach. She balked at the thought of fighting. After what Malone had said, dare she ever hit anyone again? Her vision blurred at the memory of the fight in the alleyway in front of her apartment entrance. She remembered using her carbon baton on his nuts and throat. The other she'd punched…he'd reeled backward to the corner of the Dumpster, but she'd turned away and run for the door. Which one had she killed? How could she do it differently this time?

The paralysis numbed her. Her fists clenched, but she dared not swing. She didn't want to kill an innocent policeman. For all she knew, they were just honest Ukrainian police, trying to figure out her odd behavior. She didn't want to fight them. Dared not—

Something hit the back of her head. Her ears rang, and she crumpled into blackness.

CHAPTER SIXTEEN

Abby awoke, tied to a wooden chair. She tried to see the room she was in. Not in the house, for she'd made sure she knew all the rooms and closets intimately during her time there.

And then the pounding in her head reminded her. She'd been whacked over the head with something while she'd been contemplating how not to get thrown in the cellar. She hadn't been quick enough, obviously. She was under the barn.

The walls were made of the same large hunks of stone as the farmhouse, but the ceiling was just the slatted floorboards of the barn. Chinks of light showed through the more warped and aged pieces of wood, and bits of hay poked through. There was a small sprinkling of hay on the cellar floor, which must be directly below where the hatch had opened.

But still. Tied to a chair.

She tried hard to tamp down the hopelessness she felt. Was

it fear that was prickling her skin and churning her stomach? She preferred to pretend it had been a bad oyster. Not that she'd had oysters for years, but it allowed her brain to concentrate on getting out of the dark, dank room and not on her headache and pangs of despair.

A light came on, flickering as if it had just been awoken from a long sleep. In front of her, a bare bulb swung from the ceiling. Tanoff's son opened the hatch and unfolded the wooden stairs. When he reached the bottom, he said, "*Khorosho*," to someone at the top, who pulled up the stairs again. The door of the hatch closed, and he cracked his knuckles.

"I don't understand. Why are you doing this?" As the words left her mouth, she suddenly had a bad feeling about Anton and the way he'd stared at her when he first met her, how he'd tried to get her to stay up with them the previous night. And now she knew he had tried to visit with her in her room. Well, she hoped he wouldn't do anything…unbecoming to an officer of the law. She couldn't even bring herself to admit the word she was scared of. Not scared. Never. Her fidgeting fingers behind the back of the chair told her differently.

"Doing what, Abigail?" he said in a soft voice that frankly creeped her out more than the cellar.

She nodded her head at their situation. "Is this Ukrainian hospitality? Is this how you treat guests? Volunteers?" She experimented with outrage to see if that would affect him.

His tone was conversational, as if holding her hostage, tied to a chair, was to him the equivalent to sitting opposite her at a tea party. "You see, my mother was always suspicious of you. She couldn't understand why Aide Internationale—did I say that correctly?—would send someone to them. There are, after all, orphanages with many more children in other parts of the country." He cocked his head to one side.

"My assignments are always given to me. I've never chosen them. I'm not allowed to." As the words came out, she knew she'd worded it wrongly. She'd basically made herself sound as if she were a spy. "Like your police assignments. Someone gives you jobs to do? It's the same with me." *Try to establish a rapport.* "We both have bosses to answer to, and mine thought my strength was with children—like your parents' is. We love little Dmitri, and Lana, and Anton, who they named after you." She allowed her voice and face to become soft and gentle.

It didn't work.

He drew closer. "The only question in my mind is who you are spying on here, and why. Are you an American agent, or a Russian one, or a Ukrainian? Or maybe a Chinese spy. I've heard they recruit Caucasian women to work for them."

She filed that away to tell her superiors—she hadn't heard that before.

"I'm an aid worker."

"And I'm sorry you refuse to give me what I want," he said.

She didn't know what he meant until he very softly stroked her cheek.

It took Malone another hour to reach the farm. The whole time he was trying to figure out what he could say to her, how he could apologize for being a complete and utter git. He knew that their relationship—if you could call it that—might not work in the real world. But it would be rude not to try, wouldn't it? They'd be like the biggest quitters in the world if they didn't, surely.

But by the time he got there, he'd become less certain. He was completely inexperienced when it came to relationships. How did you even start one? Was he supposed to ask her out for dinner? He had no idea. Now he wished he'd asked some of the blokes he'd been working with recently. They all seemed to do all right with the ladies.

When he crested the small hill that hid the sensor meadow from the farmhouse, it was all still silent and dark. He paused. This was a bad idea. She'd probably grabbed his phone and made her way back to her apartment. His shoulders slumped. Oh well, he'd done the walk once before.

He turned to rejoin the road to the side of the orphanage, but something moved and caught his eye. It was one of the policemen holding his weapon up and stalking across the courtyard between the barn and the farmhouse. Well, that can't be good.

Immediately his brain started filtering possibilities. He dropped to the ground and belly-crawled so he could get better eyes on the target. The barn door was open, but it looked like the policeman had come from that direction. He did a mental inventory of the things he had on him still. Binoculars and one gun. He stowed the gun where he lay. He didn't like shooting anyone who was just trying to do a legit job. There were exceptions to that, but he didn't know enough about what was going on here to make a good decision that he could live with.

The guy stopped by the kitchen door of the house and looked in, as if deciding whether or not anyone was inside. Or whether or not to storm in. God, Mal hoped he decided to stay outside. He didn't like the idea of someone with a gun being around so many children who had an inclination to wander around in the snow. But the policeman just stood, gun now at his side, as if on sentry.

So that's one at the kitchen door; maybe his friends will be at the other exits. Mal recced the house, taking his time to ensure he wasn't spotted. Yup, there was one at every egress to the property. So they'd spotted Abby? Or caught her and suspected there was someone else with her. A gut feeling told him that was it. Once he'd rounded the barn, he knew it was true. The armored vehicle was still there, meaning unless she'd decided to get the exercise of walking back to town, they had her. Or she was hiding.

He sighed. So he had to take the police out one by one. There were four total and maybe Abby's orphanage boss, depending on how entrenched he was in what was going on.

The key was silence, which was his specialty. There used to be a joke in England after the BBC showed the first-ever footage of the SAS in action, when they stormed the Iranian embassy in London, rescuing all the hostages. It was something to do with an invisible lover, trained to get in and out without anyone noticing. As it crossed his mind, he realized the joke wasn't entirely flattering.

As he always did in the seconds before being propelled into

action, he said to himself, "Who dares, wins," the motto of his old regiment. *Here's to winning.*

He caught the first man, guarding the front door, as he was lighting a cigarette. *That habit'll kill you, just not today, mate.* The guy didn't even see Mal, who held him in a choke hold until he passed out and not a second more. Mal grabbed some plastic zip ties from his pocket and tied the guard's hands between his legs. All he'd be able to do is shout by the time he came to—and by that time, hopefully it'd all be over.

The next bloke was too conveniently next to a woodpile, so Mal just crept up behind him and thwacked him on the back of the head. He crumpled without a sound.

Mal wondered if this was all going too easy—it was his nature to question ease—when the guy he'd seen earlier came upon him as he was zip-tying the second guy.

Ah, well, spoke too soon. He put his hands up and smiled and waited for the man to get closer. He did. People with guns always think they have the upper hand, but unless they shoot immediately, they rarely did.

The man motioned to Mal to turn around, which he did. But as soon as the gun prodded him in the back, Mal turned, grabbed the gun out of his grip, and threw it into the snow. The policeman was so surprised that Mal hadn't turned it on him that his gaze followed the gun instead of Mal. Big mistake.

Mal clocked him in the jaw, half power, not wanting to kill him accidentally. Unfortunately, that just reminded him of the terrible thing he'd done to Abby before he'd left the vehicle, and, distracted, he took a hard punch to the temple.

His eyes glazed over and he fought the blackness fraying the edges of his vision. He couldn't go down. Abby was depending on him to get her out. Or whatever she needed from him. If anything.

He rubbed the side of his head. "Well, that was just low and dirty. And here I was being sure not to hurt you that much. Way to make me regret my life choices, man."

The guy just looked at him, perplexed. "Ah, what the hell." He punched him straight and fast in the guy's nose. There was a crack and a spurt of blood. He hit it again, tapped it, really, and the man passed out with the pain. Mal was about to run to the barn when he stopped and corrected himself.

He turned back to the prostrate man and put him in the recovery position. Better safe than sorry. God, if his mates from the Regiment could see him now. His old mission was to plow through the enemy and get to the objective. Since he left, it was mainly up to him to decide who the bad guys were. And usually he was all right with that. But damned if putting Abby into the equation didn't eff things up for him.

He took a breath, shook his head to straighten out his vision, and made for the barn. He pressed himself against the one closed door and listened. At first he heard nothing. He remained still, patient. Then a muffled voice said something. He couldn't tell if it was a male or female voice, but it didn't sound like it was coming from the barn itself. There was no way the acoustics would be that strangled in there. He sneaked a fast look around the open door.

No shots at him, so he considered that a win, but he also saw nothing that led him to believe she was in there.

If he didn't hurry, the disabled men could rally, and no one wanted that.

He took a step into the barn and the floor creaked. He paused to see if anyone would jump out from behind the bales of hay. No one did. But when he took another step, a voice called from below the floor. *Oh, okay, so that's where she is.*

The hatch was easy to see, in a way it hadn't been when he'd first availed himself of shelter there. It had been cleared. There was no way he'd be able to sneak up on someone there, so he decided on surprise. He yanked at the metal handle and pulled it up in one motion. The stairs automatically descended, but he didn't want to risk the time it would take him to climb down.

He jumped, and it had never felt more like jumping into the pits of hell. Except in this case there was a light at the bottom. And Abby, tied to a chair. And Wank Face. He didn't know his name, and he wasn't really concerned with who he was, just that he'd tied up Mal's girl. So he was Wank Face.

Wank Face looked startled, but he backed up toward Abby, looking like he was about to put a gun to her head. "Don't even think about it, mate. You do not want to mess with me on that one."

The bastard took another step toward Abby, but to Mal's surprise—something he hid well—she leapt to her feet, such as she could, and swung her back to Wank Face so that the legs of the chair she was tied to whacked him in the nuts. Mal winced as he went down. "Come to that, you don't want to mess with her either. Lesson learned, yeah?" He grasped the front of his uniform jacket and lifted him before punching him in the face, relieving him of the pain in his balls. A mercy knockout.

"I had it handled," she said.

"Obviously." He leaned against the wooden steps and waited. "Well, come on, then, we've got to get out of here." He started up the stairs with a grin that she couldn't see. *One, two—*

"Will you stop being an ass and untie me?"

He came back down the steps and put a frown on his face. "I'm sorry, and correct me if I'm wrong, but I absolutely swear, on my mother's grave, that you just called me an ass and told me that you had all this handled." He gestured around the room and made to go up again.

"You—" She was seriously mad enough to jump up and down on the chair as if she was just trying to pull herself free.

"Ask nicely," he said.

"Please will you untie me?" she said between her teeth.

"I was thinking more along the lines of 'thank you for rescuing me; now will you please untie me, my hero? Please.' I'm not sure that's too hard under the circumstances, is it?"

"It's your fucking fault I'm here," she said, pulling at her ties again. Jesus. If she didn't stop doing that, he'd never be able to untie them. He sighed and pulled his knife out.

"What do you mean it's my fault?" he asked, sawing through the ties binding one hand. He thought he'd better get the answer before untying the second hand.

"What you told me in the car. I was too scared to fight back when they grabbed me. In case I hurt one of them." Her voice was as low as his heart was close to breaking.

He cut the second rope and pulled her up off the chair and straight into his arms. "Jesus, I'm sorry. I'm sorry for all of it. I shouldn't have told you, and if me doing that had got you really hurt, I'd never have forgiven myself."

"I'm going to remind you about that, but how about I torture you someplace else? How about we make a break for the town?"

"Deal." Getting her away from all this was what every molecule of his blood wanted to do.

No longer scared of drawing attention to themselves, they ran for the vehicle, after she'd stopped and grabbed Wank Face's gun. "I'll drive," Mal said as they reached the armored car. To ward off her objections, he rescued his phone from the corner beam and handed it to her. "You talk, I'll drive." She threw herself into the car and fastened her seat belt.

"I'm taking you back to town?" he asked as he shifted the vehicle into gear.

"Okay, but we better stay at your place. Tanoff and Brigda have my apartment address."

"Fine." And, unusually, it was. And even more unusually, he was suddenly concerned about her seeing the bare mattress on the floor, the uncultured magazines—to put it politely—and the trash he'd just thrown on the floor.

She started punching keys on the phone. "This is so much cooler than my sat phone. That pisses me off."

"Don't blame you," he said, grinning in the darkness. He wanted to tell her how amazing she'd been, but he didn't want to sound surprised that she had in fact rescued herself. To do that would be to admit he'd questioned her abilities, which he hadn't really. Dammit, things weren't this complicated with the guys in the Regiment. *But then,* a sneaky voice in his head said, *you weren't in love with any of them.*

She'd started talking on the phone, staccato bursts of information that covered the armored vehicle fake-out and the short time they were hostages. She listened to someone talking back—words Mal couldn't make out. She grabbed his arm. "We've got to go back. Turn around. Back to the border."

He carefully turned the vehicle around; as close as they were to the place where he'd taken an unseasonal dip in the ice stream, he didn't want to dunk the whole car in it too.

"Oh shit," she said to the person on the other end of the phone. "Okay, we'll sort that out afterward." After a few more affirmative answers, she hung up.

"They already have Special Forces in the air, so instead of dropping a battalion, they're dropping a couple of guys who will rig the rest of the other armored vehicles to blow. They're going to look for us at the drop point, so we better get back before they think we abandoned them."

"What was the 'oh shit' comment about? Sounds like something I should know."

She smiled at him, but then her face dropped a little. "Tanoff and Brigda, as well as her son and the rest of the local police force, are all anti-Russian. If we'd told them the truth, they probably could have helped us."

He laughed. "You can't go spilling your guts about your op to anyone just in case they're friendlies. Come on, you won't even tell your dad about your job. Why would it be okay to tell your fake employers too? Especially since they had all the guns."

She grinned. "They didn't have all the guns for long, though, did they?" She held up her hand for a high five.

He shook his head and said, "Man, you Yanks and your guns," knowing it would piss her off.

She gave him a fake stern stare and shook her hand at him, still waiting for the high five. He rolled his eyes and slapped her hand. She whooped and he couldn't stop himself from laughing. He'd never been on an op like this. Never.

"Okay, here we are," she said as they approached the glade of trees where their initial foxhole had been.

He drew to a stop and turned off the engine. There was no sign of anyone. They turned to each other and shrugged and then slowly got out of the vehicle. "Maybe we beat them here?" he said, looking at the sky.

"Doubtful," she replied. "Playboy!" she shouted, the suddenly loud noise making him jump.

"Jesus, Abby. I'm not sure how I feel about you calling me that, to be honest."

It was her time to roll her eyes. "Havoc! Playboy!" she called again.

"Okay, stop that. You sound as if you're calling your dogs in for the night."

"She kind of is, sir." A voice came from his feet and this time he did jump—literally.

Two men in combat snow gear got up, right in front of him, like they hadn't nearly given him a heart attack.

The one who had spoken introduced himself as Playboy,

and asked, "Who's the ranking?" Mal didn't bat an eye, just pointed at Abby and shook his hand. He wondered about the guy's call sign and for one irrational moment he fought not to step between Abby and the unreasonably handsome guy. Irrational because he knew you didn't choose your own call sign—they were assigned, and not usually for the obvious reason.

The second one, obviously Havoc, shook hands with both of them. "Seems we have a contrary mission, ma'am. We took off with one mission and seem to have jumped with another. Can you fill us in?"

"Sure," she said. "I've been surveilling this border area for months, waiting for any real sign of aggression that couldn't be blamed on Russian-backed rebels. These armored vehicles arrived yesterday, maybe the day before that. They seem to have taken advantage of the blizzard, parked them here and left the scene."

"So there are no troops here?" Havoc asked as he checked his tablet computer.

"Nope," Mal said. "I went up and down the line of vehicles last night and there was no one here. Judging by the lack of footprints in the snow, I think they're long gone."

"And you are…?" Playboy asked with a grin.

"A civilian who was accidently roped into this cluster-fuck by her." He pointed at Abby, who just grinned.

Playboy, trying to hide a smile, looked at Abby and then back at Mal. "I can see that happening, sir." He turned back to Abby. "Do we have a working theory on what these are doing here?"

"I think they're a distraction. I think they knew we would spot them eventually and send paratroopers and infantry to hold the border. I think the Russians are planning something bigger, elsewhere on the border."

Havoc nodded. "As we were jumping, I wondered where the tanks were. The Russians have a lot of tanks—more than the US—and they are scary beasts. If they were planning on invading from here, their tanks would be the first over the border."

"Exactly," she said. "Mal, do you want to tell them about Athens?"

Playboy's eyebrows rose. "Sir?"

Fuck it. "Sure. Okay." He turned to Playboy. "Firstly, don't call me 'sir.' I was never an officer. You can use my call sign, 'Merchant.' Secondly—"

"Merchant is your call sign?" Abby asked with a grin.

"Really? You have Playboy and freaking Havoc here and you're questioning *my* call sign?"

"Ma'am," Havoc said. "I suspect his full sign is 'Merchant of Death.' Am I right, sir?"

"You don't know him like I do. It's probably Merchant of Venice," Abby said.

"Don't make me hurt you," Mal replied, trying hard not to laugh.

"As if you could. We both know, for sure, that I can take you," she said, hands on her hips.

"Unless you lose your weapon to me, that is."

"Um, guys? I don't want to interrupt whatever this is, but— No, in fact, I do want to interrupt. Athens." Playboy looked pointedly at Mal.

"Right. We caught some Greek anarchists in bed with the Russians. They'd been planning to kidnap a Russian minister *and* blow up their own embassy. When they were being interrogated, one of them admitted that those things were planned as a distraction. Maybe this is more of the same."

They all jumped at the sound of Mal's satellite phone, which showed how on edge everyone was, despite the friendly chatter.

Mal picked up the call and handed the phone to Abby. As he did, Havoc's radio started to squawk.

CHAPTER SEVENTEEN

A bby's boss was on the line. "Yes, sir," she said.

"Whose phone is this?"

Crap. "Um, sir? It's a long story and we've got some bombing to do here." She was so getting fired.

There was silence, as if he couldn't believe her impudence. She wouldn't blame him because she couldn't either.

"Is it encrypted?" he clipped.

She turned to Mal. "Is this encrypted?"

He shrugged. "If by 'encrypted' you mean near impossible to understand, then I'd say yes. It took me a week to figure out how to send a text."

"Unclear, sir. But it's the only usable phone I have. The one I was issued died within twenty minutes of freezing temperatures. It's a good thing I wasn't trying to avert war or anything important like that." Wow. Where had the obedient operative gone? A mere week with Malone and she'd started talking like him. She kind of liked it. Especially imagining her boss's face turning beet red as it did when he was blustering.

"Okay, Baston. Rein it in." Abby pictured the alarm in his eyes as he wondered if she was going rogue.

"Yes, sir," she said, unable to keep the smile out of her voice.

"Anyway. You were right. We just got intel from Paris. A few weeks ago, the Russians accidentally assassinated one of their own ministers as he was trying to pass us some information. Our Paris office just decrypted the information. The real troop movement is occurring on two fronts: from the Crimea northward to Kiev and through Belarus to Europe. But rest assured, they will be coming back for those armored vehicles, and probably soon."

Her eyes darted around at the column of vehicles and then at Malone joking around with the two airmen. "Any idea how long we've got?"

He scoffed. "I'm not an analyst, dear. You should be in contact with your own for operational intel."

She wanted to reach through the phone…"I can't. The phone the CIA issued me died in a matter of minutes. If I hadn't found this one, none of you would have known anything until the Russians were knocking at the door of Minsk." She realized she was shouting and looked around. They were all watching her, Malone smiling, the other two apparently in shock. She couldn't bring herself to apologize, so she just hung up and called Kate.

"Oh my God, get out of there!" Kate said as she picked up the call.

"What?" Abby asked, putting her finger in one ear as if that would help her understand Kate's yelling.

"The Russians are about ten klicks away from you. They're coming back for their vehicles. I'm watching it on the infrared satellite feed. You have to go."

Abby could see Kate pacing up and down in front of her desk as she did when she was agitated. "How many are coming?"

"Abby. It looks like at least seven to ten thousand boots on the ground. Get out of there."

"Okay. On it." She hung up and faced the men. "We've got incoming."

They all looked into the peaceful sky.

"Not that kind of inbound—that kind of inbound." She pointed deep into Russian territory.

"Ma'am, did you mention Belarus?" Playboy asked.

"Yes. The Russians are planning to advance on Kiev from the south and Belarus from the east. Their plan is to push through, taking back the old soviet republics, and after that I don't know. Poland, Romania, Czech Republic. I don't know how far they'll get if we don't delay them long enough to get NATO troops mobilized."

Playboy and Havoc looked at each other. "We mobilized out of Minsk, ma'am. Our whole battalion is there, along with our unit of TACPs."

Abby nodded. "Tell who you need to tell, although I'm sure the information has already reached the forward bases, but just to be sure, you better warn them." In fact, the CIA wasn't well known for sharing intel, but she found it hard to believe they would keep information like that secret. The airmen took off to contact their people.

Malone stood before her. "You all right?" He didn't touch her in front of the airmen and she was thankful. She needed to be professional and she had a sneaking suspicion that if he hugged her, she might just break down. Tension buzzed between them.

She nodded.

"You think they'll mind that we borrowed their car? Should we stick it back with a note and some petrol money?" He looked back toward the column of vehicles.

"Maybe. I mean it'd be rude not to. Got any rubles?" She couldn't help but grin at the way he could ease the tension in any given situation, including those that ended up in her wanting to shoot out his kneecaps.

"Nah. And I guess dollars might insult them, right?"

She snorted a laugh. "Wouldn't want to do that."

The airmen came back. "We're destroying these vehicles. Want to put yours back in line? You better hurry; we're dropping five hundred pounds of shit in about six minutes."

Abby ran to the armored vehicle, cursing the idea of having to walk back to town again. And pass the orphanage. She rolled her eyes to herself. There might not be a Ukraine at all in about half an hour.

She drove it back into its place in the line and got out. And then she did tuck a dollar bill under the seat. If they inspected the remains of the vehicles, it might just confuse them. And then she had a better idea and drove the vehicle out again, parking it by the trees.

"You want to keep a souvenir?" Havoc asked as he took out two small metal boxes from his backpack.

"I'll explain later," she said, watching the two men do their thing.

Malone seemed entranced by them. She went to stand beside him. "What are you watching?"

"Me, ten years ago. I was pretty good at parachuting behind enemy lines, setting up laser targets for aircraft to lock on to, before they unleashed merry hell on the bad guys. Just so you know, the trick is to escape the area before the explosion." He took her hand in his, still looking at the airmen setting up their lasers.

"I'm not sure we have time to escape," she said, coldness seeping through her body.

"Probably not." He breathed in a puff of vapor as he squeezed her hand.

Mal watched as the two TACPs arranged their lasers and called in the strike.

Havoc messed with his tablet and then got on the radio. This took Mal back, way back, to when his only motivation was serving queen and country.

"B-one Avenger, this is Havoc."

"We read you, Havoc. We are one-four klicks from the target zone."

"Copy. Target is vehicles, marked east and west with lasers. Require a starburst pattern, five hundred pounds at a time. Do you copy?"

"Affirmative, Havoc."

The radio went silent. Playboy spoke. "Our extraction is one klick away to the south. I have instructions to bring you, ma'am. But I wasn't given any instructions about him." He nodded to Malone.

"He's coming with me," she said.

"Ma'am. There isn't enough room. As it is, you'll be taking us up to our payload max. Literally there won't be room for him."

"Then I'm staying," she said with her eyes on the lasers that Playboy had set up. "What just happened? The light on one of the lasers went out."

Havoc and Playboy started running toward the laser as they heard the faint sounds of a plane overhead.

"Shit," Mal said. "That is not good." His mind was made up. In fact, it wasn't. He didn't make a conscious decision; it was already formed in his head as the right thing to do.

He sprinted to keep up with the airmen. When he reached their side at the laser, the tripod had collapsed, leaving the laser in the melted snow. "I've got this," he said.

"With all due respect, sir, this is our job."

"With all due respect, you need to get Abby and get out of here. There is intel and ability in her that will help you win this war. I'm just a squaddie. Expendable. You have to leave me here anyway." He knew Abby was stubborn enough to stay here in front of a mighty movement of ten thousand Russian troops.

Before they could argue, he cracked open the metal box with his hands and took out the tiny frequency laser pointer. "What's its range?"

Playboy winced. "About eight meters."

"So which of you is going to essentially commit suicide here tonight, or are you going to let me do this one thing for"—*her*—"the war effort?"

"Who are you?" Havoc asked.

"Ex-SAS. She's the most valuable part of this equation. Followed by you two. If there's a war, you will be needed. I won't. Go. Get her to safety."

Havoc ripped off his protective equipment. "Lie down. Hold the laser on the side of the truck nearest to you. Dig yourself in."

Mal took a breath of relief. They understood. And Abby would, too, eventually.

"Tell her that I said she'd have to write my final report to her father for me."

"Okay, dude. I have a good feeling about this, though. I'm going to send a pararescuer back for you. He's the best, and his call sign is T.S. Don't forget that," Playboy said as he draped his own protective jacket over Mal's head.

"I won't."

"Just hold steady, and you should be fine."

"Like a rock."

Havoc kicked him lightly with his foot. "We won't forget this, Merchant. We'll go get your girl to safety."

Mal could barely hear him over the sound of the incoming aircraft. The noise soothed him, made him feel as if he were finally doing the right thing. Abby would be safe. This part of the world would be safe for now. And the young airmen would be safe.

He kept his eyes on the laser to make sure it didn't waver,

but all he saw was Abby. If he survived this, if the world survived this, he was going to get her. Her father, her job be damned.

He felt the boom of the first explosion, then the second, rattling the ground he lay on. Then he heard nothing.

CHAPTER EIGHTEEN

Abby strapped herself into the small helo that had come to extract them. Numbness pervaded her whole body. Her lower lip was the only thing moving, and she didn't know if it was because she was really cold or was about to cry. She'd been forced on board. She'd resisted for a minute but then realized she was putting the pilot's and the airmen's lives in danger by being stubborn.

She wondered if he would forgive her, because she knew for a fact that he would never have left her. She wondered if she'd ever forgive herself.

As it was, Playboy was crouching on the floor of the helo, with no safety harness because there really wasn't enough room for her in the first place.

They heard the explosions as the helo took off. She strained to see the impact the bombs had made, searching in vain, hoping to see someone run from the scene, but there was nothing. Just black smoke and the vehicles burning. Black ash floated into the sky, soiling the pristine white snow and the clear dawn sky.

As they banked away toward Belarus, something moved in the tree line. Her heart raced as she twisted in her seat to see. Had it been Mal? Russians? How would he ever get out if it had been a Russian? How would he have escaped the explosion?

Everything felt wrong. She'd made a bunch of wrong decisions. And Malone had been the victim of nearly all of them.

By the time they arrived in the forward operating base, the sun was fully up, making everything look cheerful and bright. Abby wanted everything to be dark and stormy—to match her mood.

As the helo powered down and she jumped onto the tarmac, Playboy ran over to a departing Apache. He shook a tall man's hand and pointed back at Abby. The man nodded and swung himself onto the helo just as it was taking off. Another identical Apache took off behind it, and they both powered away in the direction of the explosions.

Havoc took her over to the small terminal building to have her signed in. Playboy was FaceTiming on his cell phone. She caught a glimpse of a baby on the screen. She smiled to herself. Everyone had someone to go back to.

He hung up. "Cute. How old?" she asked, nodding to the screen.

"She was born the week before I shipped out. Perfect timing, really." A grin spread across his handsome face.

"Is your wife upset that you're here?" she asked, wondering how these relationships worked.

He snorted. "She's jealous I'm out here. She was spec-ops, ma'am, but now she's in the same line of work as you. She wants to be here in the thick of it, trust me."

"It must be nice to have someone who understands your job," she said. How many people in the world were there who would understand anything about her work? Who would be allowed to?

"It is. Anyway, we're grabbing some shut-eye before we get sent out again. I think you have to sign in here." He pointed at a desk clerk who seemed to have a huge ledger book for people arriving and departing in front of him.

"That's a little low-tech." She smiled after giving him her name.

"With all the cyber-attacks the Russians have been perpetrating, everything here is done on encrypted phones or paper. He swung the book shut and reached in a cubbyhole. "I have a message for you, ma'am."

As she opened it, Havoc poked his head out of a room. "Ma'am? The PJs that took off when we arrived—they've gone to find your friend. They'll bring him back one way or the other."

She nodded. "Thank you."

He gave her a quick smile and disappeared again.

The note told her to report to the Ops Control, and after asking directions, she made her way through a warren of cold war–style bare concrete corridors.

She arrived in a large room that looked like it could once have been a school gymnasium. In fact, now that she thought about it, the whole place was probably an old school. She'd lay bets that the tarmac where the helo landed was a sports court of some sort.

She looked at the note again and said to the first person in uniform who walked toward her, "I'm supposed to report here?"

The woman looked at the note and nodded. "You're here, ma'am. I'm just not sure who you're supposed to report to. Maybe look around until you recognize someone?"

Awesome help. And then—God. Why was nothing going her way today? Her boss, the one she'd spoken so rudely to earlier, was looking her up and down with a surprised expression.

"Sir," she said.

"I'm surprised you had the balls to actually come here, Baston. You've broken so many rules in the last week alone, I have no idea where to start."

Heat and desperation rose in her body. "You could start by thanking me for alerting you to the decoy vehicles on the border. For risking my life trying to get the message back to Langley because as it happens nearly all the equipment you sent me with was three years out of date and virtually useless. You can thank my father for worrying about me—because he thinks I'm an aid worker—and sending out a former black-ops operative to keep an eye on me. I was off book, sir. Because there is no book for what I do. The only book there is, is one for the pen pushers at headquarters. The ones who follow the rules to a T and then go home for cognac and cigars every night. I haven't even seen the USA for two years because you send me out from place to place. And I know, that's my job, but it's also my job to go off the book. I did what I needed to, to get the job done."

As she paused for breath, she realized that everyone had gone quiet in Ops Control and all eyes were on them. Her boss's face was so red, she could virtually see steam rising from its surface.

He leaned in close and said in a very low voice, "All this talk about your job is laughable, because it's up to me if you still have one. And let me tell you, as of right now, it's not looking good."

Her heart plummeted. He was firing her?

"There is a transport for Baltimore leaving in twenty minutes. You no longer have clearance to be here, so make sure you're on it. Otherwise I will cut you loose outside the security of this compound and you can make your own way back home. I hope you have your passport."

She didn't, and it didn't take her long to realize being in the capital of Belarus with no money and no passport was not the best idea. She nodded and left the room; the closer she got to the door, the more the chatter around her got louder. Dammit. She daren't risk staying here.

If the PJs found Malone, they'd look after him. Her being there wouldn't change that.

She went back to the guy she signed in with and signed out again. He directed her to a C-130 that would take her back stateside. Before she returned to the flight line, she slipped in through the door the two airmen had disappeared through. She just had to cover her bases.

Havoc was asleep on a bunk, one arm draped over his eyes and his iPhone earbuds in. She unapologetically nudged him. He awoke immediately and was alert in a way that only someone who'd slept in a war zone and had to wake up ready to pull a trigger was. He pulled out his earbuds. "S'up."

"I'm being sent back stateside. Please make them keep looking for Mal...Merchant. Don't let them give up." She scribbled her email address down on a postcard he had sticking on the wall by his bed. "Email me if they find him." She grimaced. "Either way."

He nodded. "The PJs are the best. They won't let you down. I promise."

She squeezed his rock-solid arm. "Thank you."

"No problem," he replied, already plugging his earbuds back in. But as she tuned to go, he ripped one out again. "Oh, he told me to pass this message. He said to tell you that you might have to file his final report with your father? Does that make sense?"

Tears seeped out of her eyes. She nodded and turned away.

Mal staggered into the trees, desperate for shelter after the bombs had been dropped. His vision and hearing were seriously fucked up and all he knew was that he had to find cover until his faculties returned—assuming they would sometime this side of the queen's next jubilee.

He found what felt like the foxhole he'd been in with Abby. Abby. She was going to be pissed off that he hadn't said good-bye or anything. In truth, he wanted to hold her until the world stopped. Or until the ringing in his ears stopped. Jesus. Those five-hundred pounders were brutal. And he'd been a scant few meters away from the blast zone.

He closed his eyes, put his hands over his ears, and concentrated on his breathing. His chest hurt, so he wouldn't be at all surprised to discover that he'd broken a few ribs. His arm hurt too—like a motherfucker—but he didn't care. He'd need both arms to get out of this in one piece, so he chose to ignore the fact that he might be injured.

After a few minutes, the roaring in his ears subsided a little, but he knew he couldn't rely on his hearing to figure out if the Russian fucking army was closing in. He walked out of the glade, trying to remain upright, but with his ears fucked up, his balance was all over the place.

He made it as far as the armored truck they'd borrowed. He crawled in for some respite from the cold wind. He slumped in the driver seat and saw that Abby had left some dollar bills in it. Nothing like using psy-ops on your enemy. But inside his aching brain, he knew that taking it just a little further might at least pause the invasion.

He dug out a pencil and a notepad from one of the storage areas in the vehicle and drew a crude map. He used arrows and a passable drawing of a Russian flag to show the movements of the Russian troops.

At the bottom of the map he drew the stars and stripes, and the union jack, and the European flag, with the words "we're waiting for you" in Russian. He attached the map to the headrest by anchoring it with his knife. That should give them food for thought.

He started the engine and winced as it reverberated through his body. He parked it about a hundred meters inside the Russian border and left it with all its doors open. That should get their attention.

He returned to the glade and took cover in their foxhole again. He needed to recuperate for a few minutes before trying to walk back to town. He knew the airmen had said they'd send someone for him, but he knew he wasn't official, and that despite their good intentions, they might not be able to. He wasn't going to wait around and see what kind of mood the Russians were in.

He grabbed the airmen's protective clothing and buried it in a snowdrift, not wanting to leave anything incriminating visible. As he stepped out with the intention of making it to the main road, he heard a *wop-wop* in the distance. Stepping back into the trees, he scanned the sky. It could be the PJs they'd promised, but it could also be the Russians' advance team.

The helo was coming from Belarus airspace. Once he had it in his sight and saw the markings, he stepped out. The Apache didn't hesitate. It fell from the sky at an alarming rate, leveling off when it was mere feet from the ground. Holy hell, that pilot had balls of steel.

Someone jumped out and ran toward him.

"Good morning. My name is T.S., and I'll be your rescuer today. Can you walk?"

Cocky bastard. Mal grinned and nodded, but as they made their way to the aircraft, it seemed to move farther and farther out of reach. The last thing he saw was T.S. motioning someone inside the helo, and then he checked out.

CHAPTER NINETEEN

Abby's flight back to DC was not a treat. Normally when she was heading back stateside she was excited. This time, every second she was slipping farther away from Malone, her heart died a little. And her soul cringed with the knowledge that she'd left without even knowing if he was okay. What kind of person did that? The kind of person who was under orders. She should have fucked the orders.

She realized how stupid she'd been giving Havoc her email address. He wouldn't email her about a classified mission, and she also hadn't asked him to give her contact details to Mal either. Where had her head been?

She didn't eat or drink the whole flight, not that there was a lot on offer. It was a military transit plane with virtually no one on it. She guessed most everyone was going in the opposite direction, and the plane was just heading back to Baltimore to pick up more troops. *She* should be going back. Even though she knew others were better equipped, she only wanted to go look for him.

Numbness had set in by the time they touched down at BWI. She was met at the plane by a company guy, who was escorting her to Langley, the CIA headquarters. She tried not to think about what her boss had said before she left, but facing the facts, she'd brought a civilian—no matter how capable—into an international espionage situation. No one did that and got away with it.

The escort met her eyes in the rearview mirror of the sedan. "I hear you may have averted a big European war?" he said.

"I doubt it. Delayed it, maybe." She looked out the window, hoping to signal that she didn't want to talk.

"Maybe you're getting an award," he said.

She looked at him. "More like a box with all my personal belongings in it." *Stop talking to me.*

"No way. You're a hero."

Her thoughts went back to Malone. No, *he* was the hero. He was the one who risked his life to destroy the Russian equipment that would hopefully leave the advancing Russians backpedaling.

"My boss doesn't think so," she murmured.

"But maybe *his* boss thinks so. I have directions to take you to Director Walker's office." His eyebrows rose as if to say, *How 'bout that, then?*

"Director Walker?" She looked at her clothes. She'd gotten rid of her snowsuit when she'd gotten on the plane. But that meant she was wearing jeans that had been dried out twice and a sweatshirt that had seen better days. Shit. She'd heard he was a very "proper" man, concerned with manners and decorum. She had neither going for her right now. Oh well. If you're going to get fired, may as well be from the guy at the top.

She should have been thinking about how to worm her way out of being terminated, but all she could think about was Malone. Maybe he was just lying out there, injured in the snow? What if the Russians found him before the PJs did? Maybe he died alone. Maybe he's already back in town living it up at the nearest bar, taking home some lovely Ukrainian for some comfort. Dammit. She'd never been one to indulge her imagination, but she couldn't rein it in.

She was shown straight into the director's office when they arrived at Langley. She stood awkwardly, not wanting to plant her dirty jeans on any of the elegantly upholstered chairs. For God's sake. Can't they just fire her by text or email and let her get on with her life? Not that she had a life to get back to. Not even an apartment. And how did you fill in your résumé when you only had classified things as your work experience? Shit. She was in more trouble than she thought.

Director Walker entered with purpose. He held his hand out and said, "Abigail Baston?"

"Yes, sir." She shifted her weight from foot to foot.

"Please, sit down," he ordered.

"I'd rather not, sir. I've just come in from the field, and I didn't get a chance to change clothes for a couple of days—one of which was spent in a foxhole."

"Quite. I hear you also ripped your immediate superior a new asshole." He raised his eyebrows at her.

She couldn't get past the fact that the director of the CIA had just used the word "asshole."

"I'm sorry, sir."

"Don't be. I've been trying to do it for years. Besides, we'll need that kind of straight-talking for your next assignment. You're needed in Turkey."

Turkey. Shit, that was huge. She wasn't fired. She suddenly felt pounds lighter. Turkey was such an important strategic mission, it could only be a promotion. But then her excitement seeped away. Her world was still not right.

"Sir. A civilian was involved in my last op. I had to leave him. Can you tell me if he's okay?" She stopped shifting from foot to foot, searching his face for a clue. A hint about what had happened to Malone.

"No. You should leave it alone, young lady. Occasionally we have to use all the resources at our disposal. And you did that admirably. But you have to be able to walk away too. And this is one of those times. You can't get involved with the people you meet while undercover. It will kill you as surely as a bullet. Shake it off and move on. You have two weeks to recalibrate. Read our geo briefs on Turkey. And then ship out to your new job. Keep moving. If you stop, you're dead." He swiveled in his chair and looked out the window.

"Yes, sir." She turned to go.

"My best operatives in the field are women. Twenty years

ago, you weren't even allowed in the field. The world changes, Ms. Baston. You have to keep moving with it."

"Yes, sir."

He continued to stare out at the landscaped gardens beneath his office window, so she took it as a dismissal. She left.

CHAPTER TWENTY

Mal arrived back in DC two days later. He was snatched up at the airport by Baston's driver and swept off to his boss's country pile. Baston had a huge estate in Reston, Virginia. The driver didn't give him an option of going home.

He was so fired.

"Where is my daughter?" Baston asked as soon as he got through the two sets of security checkpoints and up to the front door.

"I don't know. It's complicated," his opening salvo had been. It hadn't got any better. He couldn't tell his boss why he'd left her side. Couldn't tell him that she was CIA, couldn't tell him fucking anything. A British envoy from the Belarus embassy had visited him at his hospital bedside and reminded him that these kinds of activities were held under the official secrets act, which he'd signed some fifteen years previously, and had never expired.

"Uncomplicate it, son." He'd never in the three years he'd

worked for Baston been able to disrespect him, and now it seemed to his boss, at least, as if that was all he was doing.

"I'm sorry."

"Then tell me where she is."

"I don't know. I'm sorry."

"Let me get this straight. You were sent there to shadow her, to keep my only daughter from harm, and you come back injured with no earthly idea where she is?"

"I'm afraid so, sir."

"Is there something you're not telling me? And what I mean by that is, do you know more than you want to tell me?"

"Yes. I'm sorr—"

"You are on house arrest here until you tell me where. My. Daughter. Is." He was shouting as he punctuated his last words with a stabbing pointer finger, and Mal didn't blame him.

"I'm sure she's safe," he offered.

"You're sure. One hundred percent sure? Or you think?"

"I think."

"Then you won't be leaving until I get to the bottom of this. Go." He nodded toward a security protection officer who had silently entered the office.

"Mr. Garrett. Please follow me."

And so he'd stayed there. Two days and counting. People had come in to ask him what he knew. But he couldn't tell them anything. Doctors came and went. Drugs were administered for pain and inflammation and for his broken ribs and arm. And he slept in discomfort, his dreams peppered with images of Abby.

He could have left at any time; he could escape with relative ease. But he wanted to know the second Baston had been in contact with Abby. And this was by far the best place to be to stay in the loop. He prepared himself to never see her again. The nature of her business meant that she would always move on and start a new life. He had hoped, in his most miserably painful moments in the hospital, that she might—what? Quit her job? On the basis of a weeklong combative relationship? He was crazy. It might even have been the drugs. There was no future for them, and for the first time in his life—the first time ever—he was inexplicably heartbroken.

Even David Church, the guy he'd met in Greece, had stopped by to chat. He'd been supposed to interrogate Mal, but they'd just chatted about what he'd been up to since Greece. Baston had sent him on a few missions, but he'd always flown back to his girlfriend instead of his own home. It was sweet, really. The most effed up man he'd met on the job had found a perfect girl, *and* in the course of a mission.

Where *was* Abby?

Abby had spent three whole days looking at geopolitical intel about Turkey. She'd looked at it for hours, but actually hadn't read any of it. As soon as she tried to concentrate on the words on the document, her thoughts flittered away to Malone.

Where *was* he?

By the afternoon of the third day, she'd come to a decision. She needed answers. Needed to see him, or she'd never be able to concentrate on her next assignment. And then she looked at the table full of information, and for the first time felt no enthusiasm, no spark or excitement. Mal had taken away any positive feeling when he'd decided to leave her and be the hero.

She needed him. Needed to know he was okay. Alive. She just needed to know. And there was only one person who could help. She agonized over it for all of thirty seconds and then she grabbed her purse and the keys to her rental car and ran from the hotel.

It took her twenty minutes to get to Reston and another ten to make it through the security checkpoints. Each minute that ticked by increased the pressure on her heart. Why hadn't she done this on her first day back? Her first hour?

She parked the car dead in front of the entrance, knowing her father would be pissed and not caring.

She rang the bell. Seriously? Even though security had to have advised him that she was coming, he still made her wait.

At least he answered the door himself and hadn't sent one of his men to do it.

"Abigail. Where have you been?" If she didn't know what a hard-ass he was, she would have sworn that he was choked up.

"I've been in the Ukraine. You know that. You sent someone to spy on me."

He hustled her into his first-floor office—more of a library with bookshelves lining the walls, only she knew that they weren't really all books. Some were containers; some hid false doors. It was a kid's paradise. Her mouth twitched as she remembered exploring it when they'd first moved there.

"How do you know I sent someone?" he asked, chopping the end of his cigar in a pocket guillotine.

"Where is he? Have you heard from him? Did he make it

out? Pops. Tell me." She would have grabbed him if he hadn't put the desk between them.

He frowned at her. "You mean him?" He pointed at the door they'd just come in. She turned.

Malone was standing just inside the door, one arm in a sling and bruises over one side of his face. Relief took the air from her lungs, and she bent over just trying to breathe. "Thank God." An embarrassing moan of disappearing tension came out, too, but she just didn't care. "Malone."

In a second he was at her side, crushing her in a one-armed hug.

"Well, this is very interesting," her father said.

Neither of them paid attention to him.

Her father cleared his throat, and they pulled apart. She grabbed his hand, though, not wanting to let go of him. "How the hell did you survive that explosion?" she asked, willing the welling tears back into her eyes. "It was like Armageddon down there. I couldn't imagine how you'd get out. And then no one told me where you were, or even if you were alive." She closed her eyes and swallowed. Then she opened them and punched his good arm.

"Ow. That's not very nice."

"Why didn't you call me?" she demanded.

"How was I supposed to do that? The white pages? I don't even think that exists anymore. You didn't give me any way to get in contact with you. Your father has been interrogating me every hour to find out where you were." He sounded pissed, but he was grinning and stroking her hand with his thumb.

Her father butted in. "Question is, why didn't you call me to tell me you were okay? That's a better question."

"Pops, if you're trying to spy on me—or rather by having someone else spy on me, which is worse—you can't complain when your own operative loses track of me."

"Way to throw me under the bus, love. Thanks very much," Mal said, shaking his head in mock disappointment.

"Knowing you, you'd survive being run over by a bus, so I'm not worried."

Baston raised his voice. "Enough. Someone tell me what's going on here. So help me, if you and my daughter—"

"Pops, sit down," Abby said, sitting on one of the leather chairs by his desk. "I'm CIA. I'm a CIA operative. I was working in Ukraine, watching for the Russians. They came, and Mal helped me get word back to Langley…and here we are."

Her father sat down abruptly and chewed on his cigar, which he still hadn't lit. Now that she'd told him, she guessed she'd have to quit the Agency. A weight lifted from her. Maybe she should have done this years ago.

"Ex-CIA, I guess," she said. "As soon as I hand in my resignation."

"Really?" Mal said. "So you'll be sticking around here?"

She shrugged. "I haven't really thought it through. I literally made up my mind to quit thirty seconds ago."

"Come and work for me," her father said, not missing a beat.

She looked at him, flabbergasted. "Really? That's the first thing you think when I tell you I've been working for the CIA? Not, 'how could you have lied to me?' not 'my dearest

baby girl, have you been in danger?' but 'come work with me'?"
She shook her head.

"I'm a businessman, sweetheart. If there's someone sitting in front of me with Agency training, who's suddenly out of a job, it's my patriotic responsibility to offer her a job. To insist on it. Besides, having a female operative would widen my business hugely." He finally lit the cigar and bellows of blue smoke wafted between them. "Not to mention a pair of operatives who can pose as a married couple."

She looked at Malone, who was grinning widely and not saying a word. She grinned back.

"Well, you bicker like an old married couple, anyway. So you have that going for you."

"Permission to steal her away for a minute, sir?" Malone jumped to his feet and held his hand out for hers.

She grabbed it and stood.

Her father groaned. "Don't make me...I don't want to know." He raised his voice as they left the room. "Not under my roof."

She giggled as Malone took the stairs two at a time, dragging her behind him. "What's the rush?" she gasped.

"We have a lot of practicing to do before we can go undercover as a married couple. A whole lot."

EPILOGUE

Two years later

They'd just wrapped up their fifteenth mission as a married couple. After the seventh mission, they actually made it official by getting married on a Caribbean island, as part of their cover. They thought getting married while on a mission was perfect. Perfect for them anyway.

Any talk of war had been delayed. Officially the Russians had entered into negotiations with the EU. Unofficially, word had got back that NATO knew their game plan and they'd beat a fairly hasty retreat to lick their wounds. So all was quiet until it happened again, which these things usually did.

And now Mal and Abby were on their way to their sixteenth mission—the most important one of their lives. Baston had sent them in his private jet. Abby was nervous. Mal could tell by how utterly still she was. She was literally the opposite of anyone he'd known. She went still and calm when she was nervous, and she was alive and buzzing when she was at ease. It had been the pleasure of his life to discover these little parts of his wife that few other people could see.

"It's going to be fine," he said, wrapping his arm around her.

"You're not nervous?" she asked, examining his face for weakness.

"Of course I am. It's only natural. But everything will work out brilliantly. You'll see."

"Care to take my mind off it?" she asked with a raised eyebrow.

"Abso-bloody-lutely," he said. "As long as your father doesn't have a camera on board."

"I had them taken out before we boarded," she answered with a sly smile.

"That's why I love you. You're always prepared." He grinned and stood.

"Yes, I am." She unzipped her sweatshirt and showed him what was underneath.

He took in her navy blue lingerie and sighed. "You're *so* much better than a Boy Scout."

"Yes, I am," she repeated, unzipping her denim skirt and letting it fall to the floor.

She stepped out of it and put one knee on the sofa that stretched the length of the aircraft. "Where do you want me? Here?" She stroked her hand along the arm of the sofa. "In the galley?"

In an instant he visualized her sitting on the stainless steel galley, legs around his head as he licked her until she came. His dick was already hard at the thought of her softness. He picked her up, making her squeal, and strode into the galley, depositing her on the metal countertop.

"Cold," she whispered.

"Very, very hot," he countered, slowly pushing her knees open until her panties strained against her. He dipped his head and licked the length of her over the blue silky material. She leaned back and pushed into him, wriggling against his tongue. He eased his finger under her panties and ran it over her clitoris, using her own wetness to make her squirm. His tongue still laved the material in broad strokes. He was desperate to taste her properly but loved to tease her into submission.

"Who's your boss?" he asked in between strokes.

"You are, you bastard," she moaned.

"You know it, love." He used his finger to slip the material to one side so that his tongue stroked against her clit.

She moaned, making his dick strain against his trousers. He took a second to undo his belt and let them fall to the ground. Abby undid his shirt and raked her nails over his chest, making his nipples throb in tandem with his dick.

He drew his tongue around her clit and slipped two fingers into her, curling them slightly. He stroked inside her, feeling her tighten around him. She was close. He sneaked a look at her, flushed, mouth slightly open, eyes closed, totally lost in his touch. He adored seeing her like that.

She flicked open her bra in the front and with one hand still bracing herself on the counter, began to play with her own nipple. He was about ready to explode himself. He stood up, put his mouth around her other nipple, and bit gently, then licked it and blew cold air across it, making it hard. He moved his thumb to her clit and thrust his fingers in and out. She clenched, and just as she was about to come, he bit her nipple again. Her orgasm seemed to settle over her whole body, shaking as it subsided.

She wrapped her hands around his neck and he lifted her down.

"It's your turn now, baby," she purred.

"I already know exactly how I want you." He turned her around and bent her over. He could see her face and breasts reflected in the mirrored backsplash. Still in her high-heeled shoes, she wiggled a little as she spread her legs for him. He entered her with one thrust. She gasped and pushed back at him. He reached around her and watched himself play with her nipples as he pushed inside her. Heat pulsed out from his lower back, and with a few thrusts his balls tightened and he paused for a second, loving the feeling of being inside her, being part of her, and with his eyes on his wife's face, he came, shuddering inside her.

"I love you, Mrs. Garrett," he said as he wrapped his arms around her.

"You better," she gasped back.

With incredible timing, the pilot came over the intercom. "Ten minutes to landing."

They stood up and she turned to face him. "A fine impression we'll make like this."

"Half of me wants to fly naked with you. Like always. So I can touch you for the whole flight."

"Wrap it up, pal. We usually fly commercial." She fastened her bra and grabbed her sweatshirt and skirt.

"Well don't you just spoil all my fun." He grinned as he pulled up his pants.

"Do I?" She arched an eyebrow at the galley.

"Valid point. Naked flying a topic for another conversation."

She brushed past him and whispered in his ear, "Or another role play."

He held his fist out and she bumped it. God, he loved this woman. She was the perfect dichotomy of pure balls and all woman. She constantly surprised him, and today she was making him the happiest man in the world.

Someone new was joining their team.

After they disembarked at the general aviation part of the airport, where the private planes were received, she searched for a familiar face.

This was the icing on the cake for her, the perfect result of their mission in Ukraine, her meeting what turned out to be the love of her life, and for them both to return here, to find the love of both their lives.

Tanoff waved as they came through security. He kissed her on both cheeks and shook Mal's hand with vigor. Next to him, Brigda held a sleeping eight-month-old baby in her arms. Tears welled in Abby's eyes, and this time she let them fall. Brigda smiled and carefully put the baby in her arms. There was a flash as Mal took a photo. "It's one of you crying, not of our daughter or anything." It was one of his usual smart-ass remarks, tempered by the very soft voice he said it in as he peered down into the bundle of blankets and stroked his new daughter's face with his finger.

She had made contact with Tanoff when she and Mal had

been married a year. They'd discussed a family and had decided that since they had firsthand knowledge of the orphanage, they would adopt a child from them. Since the toddlers she'd worked with had already been adopted, they'd waited for a child who had no one.

Seven months ago they'd got the call, and after all the paperwork had been done and stamped in what seemed like fifteen different offices in the US and Ukraine, they'd set off on their final—for now—husband-and-wife mission.

"Perfection," Mal murmured.

"She is," Abby replied.

Her husband looked into her eyes. "I meant my world."

About the Author

Emmy Curtis is an editor and a romance writer. An expat Brit, she quells her homesickness with Cadbury Flakes and Fray Bentos pies. She's lived in London, Paris, and New York and has settled, for the time being, in Germany. When not writing, Emmy loves to travel with her military husband and take long walks with their Lab. All things considered, her life is chock-full of hoot, just a little bit of nanny. And if you get that reference... well, she already considers you kin.

Learn more at:
EmmyCurtis.com
Facebook.com/EmmyCurtisAuthor
Twitter: @EmmyCurtis19

Turn the page for an excerpt from *Compromised*, available now!

One year ago

Y ou got laid last night, didn't you?" Simon Tennant asked as he recognized the look on his friend's face. He'd seen it many times before. A cross between "holy hell, I'm lucky" and "what the fuck did I just do?" "I don't know how you do it, man."

Matt Stanning grinned as he fastened his seat belt. "Gotta love weddings," he said. "They make chicks crazy."

"But mine? You couldn't keep it in your pants until I was safely on my honeymoon? You better not have hit and quit one of Sadie's friends, or I'll never hear the end of it!" He was lying. His fiancée had a soft spot for Matt. In truth, Sadie had a soft spot for a lot of people; it was one of the things he loved about her.

Simon took a deep breath, barely believing *still* that she was about to become his wife. A sense of peace was blooming in his body, almost as if he were dying and being drawn to the light. No wait—way wrong analogy. He came up empty for anything better. He checked his watch. In four hours, Sadie Walker would become Mrs. Simon Tennant, and his life would finally be complete.

She was his anchor in the crazy world he worked in. The calm in the storm that raged through his professional life. After every mission, his only focus was getting home to her. Home. Sadie. He needed her in his life like a fire needs oxygen. He'd always thought that having a significant other would dull his desire to take the fight to the enemy, but that never happened. If anything, knowing he had her to come home to made him a better operative. Simply, his life was exponentially better with her in it. And he was about to make that permanent.

"So who was it?" He flashed a look at Matt, whose smile faltered just a little.

"You know, I'm not even sure she gave me her right name. Harry? Henrietta? Something like that." Matt was frowning now.

"She's Sadie's maid of honor. Her friends call her Harry," Simon said as he shifted down to turn on the road to Sadie's parents' house. He was a little intimidated to be in the home of the director of the CIA. As if getting married wasn't nerve-racking enough.

"Funny, she told me I should call her Henrietta."

Matt looked so perturbed Simon couldn't help but laugh. He was about to explain a little about her history, when he noticed the security barriers in the middle of Sadie's driveway were up, rendering it impassable.

"What's going on?" Matt asked as Simon pulled on the hand brake and got out of his car.

"No idea." Behind him he could hear Matt getting out of the car too.

"Excuse me," he called to a patrolling security man in black.

The man did a double take and looked around him as if seeking assistance. Then he placed his hand on his sidearm and approached the gate.

"Something's not right," Simon said in a low voice to Matt. Matt stayed silent.

"Can I help you?" the security man said in a careful voice.

"Hi there. Can we come in?"

"No one is allowed. Private. Come back later." The security man was sweating.

Simon could sense that Matt was about to explain that Simon was the groom, so he cut in. "Okay, no problem. We'll come back this afternoon."

They got back into the car and Simon threw it into reverse and slowly backed down the driveway. He rolled down his window and put the radio on loudly. As soon as he did that, the security man turned and walked away. There was nothing like music to divert attention and suspicion.

"Ukrainian?" Matt asked.

"I'd say southern Russian. He's not a member of the director's security team or the family's. Something's wrong."

Simon's Delta Force training immediately took over. He turned to Matt. "I'm going in."

Matt didn't hesitate. He shrugged out of his jacket and rolled up his sleeves. "How do you want to play this?"

"Not quite sure yet, but at least I've brought some toys to the party." Simon flashed a wolfish grin.

"Music to my ears."

Simon parked the car far enough up the road that it was out of sight from the house. They jumped out as Simon popped the trunk with his fob and pulled aside the floor to reveal an array of small weapons.

"Dude, you shouldn't have," Matt said as if he'd been presented with the best gift ever.

Simon wanted to laugh, but in truth, he had only one thing on his mind and he was deadly serious about it: Get to Sadie. "Take extra ammo and the silencers. We have no idea how many of them there are."

They took their weapons of choice. "Are you absolutely sure we're not going to scale the wall and jump down in the middle of your mother-in-law-to-be's garden party?" Matt said.

It was possible. But his gut told him different. "You haven't met Sadie's mom. This would also be an entirely appropriate reaction to her." He chambered a round and held Matt's eyes. "You sure you're okay with this?"

Matt looked away, unconcerned. "Hey, this is what we do. Let's go get our girls."

Simon nodded once and the two approached the wall around the property, smoothly scaled it, and started scoping out the grounds as they made their way to the house. Sadie was in there.

His Sadie. If anything happened to her…

Simon slid around the side of the wedding tent in the backyard. As he rounded the front, he found two men, guns holstered and smoking. He showed himself, just on the slim chance that they were the director's guards. They went for their guns immediately, and he shot both of them in the forehead, barely registering the hits. He swung around instinctively to cover his back, but no one was there. He dragged the two men into the tent and closed the front flaps.

"Delta Lima, check in," a voice said over the walkie-talkie fastened to one of the men's belts. Answer or not answer?

Simon took a breath. "Da."

There was a long pause, and then the person at the other end clicked his SPEAK button in acknowledgment.

The tent flap moved, and he nearly took a shot. It was Matt. He needed to get a fucking grip on his emotions is what he needed to do right now.

"There are two on the right side of the house. One has a tablet or something that he seems to be monitoring. He's our mark, the one we need to question," Matt said, casting his eyes over the dead men on the ground.

"Copy that. It'll be my pleasure," Simon replied. The faster they got this done, the faster he could get to her. *Damn it—why didn't we elope?*

He exited the tent first. The lawn area was still empty. He ran for the house, so they could take the two men without the exposure of a direct approach. The guards were so focused on their tablet that Simon felt they could have just ambled up and asked them the time. Still, where was the fun in that?

He rounded the corner. "Hi there," he said.

About eight minutes later, they were inside the house, Simon taking the final kill-shot to end the immediate danger.

"Where's Sadie?" he asked her brother, James. James pointed to the corridor behind him and Simon didn't hesitate. He needed eyes on her. As he approached her bedroom, she emerged, fear etched on her face.

"Oh my God, Simon. Thank God. I didn't know..." She dissolved into sobs that she stifled against his neck. His arms went around her. He was never letting her go. Never letting her out of his sight.

"Simon, we need you," James said. "My father is still in his study with two of the gunmen."

He looked up; Matt, James, and James's fiancée were all locked and loaded, waiting at the top of the stairs for him. "I have to go."

"No—don't leave me. Please don't leave—" she begged, and his heart just about cracked open. But Simon had no choice. It was his duty.

"I'll be right back. I promise."

She pulled away from him, makeup running down her face. "I can't, Simon. This..." she gestured at the dead man. "I can't..."

"Look at me. I'll be right back." He kissed her on the forehead and stalked down the corridor toward the others. He looked back as they took the stairs. She was hugging her younger sister, eyes squeezed shut, sobbing. A part of his heart fell away into darkness. Who would leave anyone suffering like that, let alone the woman he loved? But he had a duty. A duty to protect the United States from enemies, foreign and domestic. And country came first. Always.

Didn't it?

Ten minutes later, all the bad guys had been disposed of, but Sadie's brother had been shot. Simon ran from the scene to Sadie, but she was already outside staring at the dead bodies in the exact place they would have said their vows. One look in her eyes told him that they weren't going to get married that day.

"Sadie, please—just listen," he said, preempting anything that was going to come out of her mouth.

"I can't. I'm sorry. I see now what you do every day that you're not with me. This is what you do every time you leave me." She pointed at the knocked-over flower arrangements and the bloodstained aisle carpet.

"Please, I just need to explain—" An ambulance's sirens interrupted his plea.

Sadie's eyes flashed with horror. "Who...?" She looked at the front door.

Simon cursed himself. "I'm sorry; James was shot. I think he'll be fine, though."

"What?" She took a deep breath and then swallowed. "I have to go see him."

"I know." He could feel the distance between them already. He'd been worried about this the whole time they'd been dating. He never told her exactly what he did on a day-to-day basis. And now he'd never have to. It was here, in her family home, the dead bodies and blood that she would never be able to unsee.

"We'll talk. Later maybe," she said softly.

He reached in to kiss her goodbye, but she flinched away, shattering his heart into a million dark pieces. Suddenly he was alone, ice cold, with blood on his hands. Literally.

In that second, he knew with absolute certainty. No matter how much they'd talk, it would end the same way.

* * *

Sadie watched the nurses and doctors flit about the ICU with a detachment that she fought against. She needed to be here for her brother. Mentally and emotionally here.

She knew that no matter what she and Simon said, whatever they would discuss, it was over. The blood, his ability to leave her when she begged him not to, the *blood*. She'd known that he was in the black ops field of the army since the day she'd received her beautiful engagement ring, but now she'd seen him kill someone. Without giving his victim a second look. And then she'd gone outside and seen the blood all over the floorboards, carpet, and chairs where they'd expected to take their vows—she looked at her watch—two hours ago. There couldn't really be a clearer sign that this was not meant to be.

"Hey." His voice made her jump.

She looked up at him for a long time, not knowing what to say, where to start. Just seeing him there brought tears to her eyes. She had loved him so much. Maybe she still did, but his job was so dangerous, and so brutal, how long would it be before he was killed or something would happen that would change things for them forever? And even if it didn't, he would always be leaving her. He already treated his job as his wife and Sadie as his mistress, and now she knew for sure what he'd always left her for: death and destruction.

"Is he okay?" Simon asked as he sat next to her.

She nodded, looking straight ahead at the nurses' station, not daring to meet his eyes in case she just threw herself into his arms.

"But we're not, are we?" he said.

Sadie couldn't bring herself to nod or shake her head. Any movement would take the conversation somewhere she didn't want it to go, couldn't bear it to go.

"What happened? Look at me, dammit," he said, pain in his voice. "You can't just cut and run on our wedding day."

She took a deep breath, praying her voice wouldn't break and her chin wouldn't quiver, and turned toward him. "You cut and run all the time. When I had the flu, when we were just about to leave to go to Samantha and Jake's wedding, when we were supposed to take that vacation to Santa Barbara...movie dates, dinner dates. Your cell phone would chime and I knew I'd be on my own again. And I didn't mind too much. I knew you had an important job. But..." She swallowed, trying to keep her shit together. "Now I know what you do. Every time you leave me, it was to go kill someone, walk into danger...and I can't compete with that—I don't even want to."

Simon was silent, his eyes searching hers.

She blinked slowly and turned back around to face the nurses' station again. The nurse who had rushed James into the operating room appeared but didn't look at Sadie. When the nurse disappeared again, she turned back to Simon.

He was gone.

For a second she couldn't breathe, and then oxygen stuttered through her lungs and heaved out once, as sobs came from her stomach, her soul. He never once hesitated to fight for his country, but he refused to fight for her. She shook, and wept, and couldn't stop.

Not for a long, long time.

CPSIA information can be obtained
at www.ICGtesting.com
Printed in the USA
FFOW02n1216220816
26936FF